SHARON G. FLAKE

SCHOLASTIC INC.
New York   Toronto   London   Auckland
Sydney   Mexico City   New Delhi   Hong Kong

ISBN 978-0-545-29641-0

Text copyright © 2005 by Sharon G. Flake. All rights reserved. Published by Scholastic Inc., 557 Broadway, New York, NY 10012, by arrangement with Disney•Jump at the Sun Books, an imprint of Disney Book Group, LLC. SCHOLASTIC and associated logos are trademarks and/or registered trademarks of Scholastic Inc.

12 11 10 9 8 7 6 5 4 3 2   11 12 13 14 15/0

Printed in the U.S.A.   40

First Scholastic printing, September 2010

Lexile is a registered trademark of MetaMetrics, Inc.

For Alvera Johnson,
Gwen Evans,
and several of the men in their lives:
Patrick Evans,
Charles Linton,
James Linton,
Corden Porter,
Brandon Radford,
and
Jesse Johnson

To Cassandra Allen
and the man in her life, Ryan
For Suzanne Davis and her men, Chuckie and Little Chuck
And to Francine Taggert and her two fine men,
Charles and Charles Ross

It has been a pleasure having you in my life and
witnessing the fruit of your love.

Boys Ain't Men . . . Yet

Boys ain't men . . . yet.
They are sneakers with strings untied
Broken bikes and blackened eyes
Fast footraces and dirty faces
But they ain't men, not yet.

Boys ain't men . . . yet.
They are stolen kisses from a young girl's cheek
Sagging pants strutting up the street
Homework turned in two days late
Video wizards and basketball greats
But they ain't men, not yet.

Boys ain't men . . . yet.
They are skirt chasers and moneymakers
Late-night rides, muscles and pride
Prom dates handing out flowers and grins
Ready to take on the world and win
But they ain't men, not yet.

Boys ain't men . . . yet.
They are tall, giant reeds, trying to survive
Strong arms pushing trouble aside
Corner sitters, watchers and seekers
On the lookout for men willing to lead 'em.

—Sharon G. Flake

HEY KILL PEOPLE where I live. They shoot 'em dead for no real reason. You don't duck, you die. That's what happened to my brother Jason. He was seven. Playing on our front porch. Laughing. Then some man ran by yelling, "He gonna kill me. He's gonna—"

Before the man finished saying what he had to say, a boy no older than me chased him up our front porch steps. The man yelled for Jason to get out the way. But Jason just stood there crying. Right then, the boy pulls out a gun and starts shooting.

1

Bang! Guns really sound like that, you know. *Bang!* And people bleed from everywhere and blood is redder than you think. *Bang!* And little kids look funny in caskets. That's 'cause they ain't meant to be in one, I guess.

My brother died two years ago. But I can't stop thinking about him. And I can't walk in the house through the front door no more because of the blood. My mother says it's gone. "See?" she says, pointing to the porch floor and the gray wooden chairs. "Long gone." But I can still see it. I can. So I come into the house through the back way. Stepping over the missing stoop Jason used to put his green plastic soldiers in. Opening the iron gate that my dad put up to keep trouble out. Going inside the house and not looking at my brother's room, because if I even see his door, I cry. And a thirteen-year-old boy ain't supposed to cry, is he?

The day Jason died I was with Journey—a horse. She stays at Dream-a-Lot Stables, not far from where I live. It's a broke-down stable where kids hit her with rocks and try to make her eat sticks. But my father, he taught me and Jason to ride Journey, and brush her good. So even though she ain't ours, Journey likes us best. The man who owns the stables and rents out broke-down horses for five bucks an hour would let us ride for almost free, long as we cleaned Journey's stable first. So that morning, after my mom and dad went to work, I left Jason home by hisself. I walked to the stables and brushed the flies and dirt off Journey's blond coat. I swept up turds as big as turtles, and rode Journey all the way home—up the avenue and past Seventh Street, between honking cars, slow buses, and grown-ups who patted her butt, then got mad when she broke wind in their faces.

When I got home, Jason was on the porch. He asked me to play toy soldiers with him. I wouldn't. Journey was thirsty. So I went around back to get a hose so she could drink. That's when I heard the man yelling, and Jason screaming my name. I ran to the front of the house. The boy chased the man up our steps and onto our porch. Journey shook her head and stomped her feet on the pavement. The gun went off. The hose in my hand soaked the porch, squirted the dead man and splashed blood everywhere. Neighbors tried to pull it away from me, but I wouldn't turn it loose. That's what they say anyhow.

After Jason was gone, I saw a psychologist for six months. But my father didn't like that, so I quit going. "You a man, not no sissy baby girl," he said when he found me one day behind the couch, crying.

My mother got mad at him. "I'm gonna cry over my baby boy till I die," she said, hugging me. "Guess Mann here's gonna cry awhile too."

My father used to be in the army, so he don't cry much. And he don't want no boy crying all the time neither. That's what he tells me anyhow.

A week ago my mother told my father I needed help. "We all do," she said, sitting down on the living-room floor next to me. "It's been nearly two years since Jason died, and it hurts like it happened this morning."

My father stood behind his favorite brown leather chair. "I don't need no help. And him," he said, pointing to me, "ain't nothing that momma's boy needs but a good old-fashioned butt-kicking."

I am not a momma's boy, but since Jason died, that's what my dad calls me. "People die," he said. "Little people die too. Get over it."

My mother jumped up. Her knee knocked me in the chin. I held my mouth, because I bit my tongue and I didn't want her feeling bad about that. "So you're over it, huh?" she said, running up to the window and pulling back the white curtains. "Yeah, right," she said, holding on to the heavy, iron bars that cover every window and door in our house.

My mother walked past my father and unlocked the drawer to his desk. She picked up his .38 and stuck her arm high in the air like she does when she's hailing a cab. Then she reached in the drawer with her other hand and pulled out a rusty hunting knife big enough to cut your arm off. "He cries," she said, looking at me and pointing the gun at my father, "but you, you—"

"Shut up, Grace. I'm warning you."

My mother kept talking. Next thing I knew my father was pulling his gun and knife out her hands and locking them back in the drawer. She hugged him from behind. "He didn't deserve to die. He was sweet and smart and gave hugs when you—"

My dad covered his ears with his hands. *"Grace!"*

She ran to the window and yelled out. "You killed us too! We look like we still alive but we dead. Rotten inside." She punched her flat stomach. Bit down on her arm. "Ja. . . Ja. . ."

My father shook her. "Don't say his name! Don't ever—"

My mother's eyes are big red circles with black bags under 'em that won't go away since Jason died. "He's gonna be nine in a few months," she said. "We have to make a cake. Buy him something special."

My dad spit at the trash can. Some made it in. The rest stuck to the outside like a slug. "A dead boy don't need no presents. I told you that last year."

We always get cakes on our birthdays. And we always sing songs and make the day extra special, not just for me and Jason, but for my mom and dad too. My mother says it wouldn't be right to leave Jason out now. So she gets him presents he can't open and makes him cakes he can't eat.

My dad said what my mother never wants to hear. "Grace. He's gone. And he ain't never coming back."

I watched her, 'cause I knew them words were gonna get her too sad to make supper, or laugh when the funny shows came on TV tonight.

My mother went to the front door and opened it wide. Then she ran onto the porch and yelled for Jason. My dad ran after her. But by the time he got there, she was on her knees picking up little green soldiers we find on the porch sometimes but can't figure out just how they get there. She stomped her feet. "Jason. You come home. Come home right now!"

My father kneeled down beside her. He rubbed her lips, then covered up the rest of her words with his fingers. And then he cried, right along with her.

Chapter 2

THREE DAYS LATER my father apologized. He said he was sorry for making my mother so upset. Sorry for saying all them things about Jason. She was glad he said it. After that, they got dressed and went to the movies. I went to my room and tried to figure out why she couldn't figure out that tomorrow he was gonna say them same things all over again.

"He can't help it," she says all the time. "He just doesn't know what to do with all the things he's feeling inside."

7

I know she's right. Only I get tired of him being mean. He used to be different. He used to take us to the park. Slide down snow hills with us and lie in bed between me and Jason and make up stories about two boys walking from here to China. Then Jason died and so did my dad, kinda.

One time, when my mother and him were arguing about the way he treated me, she made me go get some of Jason's things. I walked over to the middle bookshelf and picked up Jason's lunch box—the one he had in his hand that day he got killed.

"Give it here," my mother said. She opened it. Took out the note. "'Daddy loves you.'"

My father snatched the napkin out her hand and tore it up.

My mother pointed to a Buster Brown shoe box sitting way on top of the bookshelf. "I still got the rest," she said, talking about the other notes my dad had put in Jason's lunch box. *Have a nice day*, they'd say. *Meet me after school for coffee*, he'd write. Only he never gave Jason real coffee—just grape juice in a coffee mug. "Us men have to have something strong now and then," he'd say. That always made Jason laugh.

I got notes every day too, when I was Jason's

age. But when I turned nine, they stopped. My father took me to the yard right after my birthday party that year, and burned them. "What's between a father and his son," he said, putting one hand on his heart and the other on mine, "can't be burned by fire, washed away by water, or destroyed with human hands." He squeezed me so hard, I couldn't breathe. Then he gave me a note—the same note he gives me every year on my birthday. *What we have is forever* it says. When I was ten, I got to hold on to the note for ten hours. At thirteen, I kept it for thirteen hours. When my time's up, I give it back to him until my next birthday. I always liked getting that note. But I don't believe it no more.

 DON'T WANT TO go to school no more. But I go. And I put out the trash every Wednesday night, shovel the pavement when it snows, walk my mom to the corner store when it's dark out, and clean up the house without nobody even asking. I started doing everything right once Jason died, 'cause my mom couldn't take no more trouble. Only the closer it gets to his birthday, or the day he was shot, the more I can't do like I promised her—make it so she never got a reason to cry over me too.

The only one who knows how I really feel about

stuff is Kee-lee. We walk to school together. We tease Keisha, a girl Kee-lee likes, and get on our teachers' nerves asking questions that don't have nothing to do with the classes they're teaching.

"I ain't going," Kee-lee says when I get to his house. He lives up the street from me. We supposed to be headed to school, like every morning. He takes a smoke from behind his ear and lights up. "I'm tired of school."

I sit down on the new rocker his mother bought off a man driving a truck full of frozen chicken and steaks, gold chains, hats, and porch furniture. "You always saying that."

Kee-lee can hold smoke in his mouth a long time, so it takes him a while to answer. "My mom says I can quit school if I want." He walks past me with no shirt on and sits on the front steps in his horse-head pajama bottoms. "Hey, Keisha," he says, calling to her across the street. "Want some of this?" He shows her his tongue.

Her middle finger goes up. "Brush your rotten teeth, stank mouth." She goes back into her house. Kee-lee laughs and says he knows she likes him.

When Kee-lee smiles you see green sitting right next to yellow, and thick white clumps packed close to the gums like hard sugar. Girls don't say hi when he walks up to them. They say, "Ill. Brush your teeth." He brushes them now. But it's too late. The stuff won't come off. Him and me tried. We used a fingernail file once. It made his gums swell up and bleed.

We get back to talking about school, and Kee-lee says he's dropping out for sure. That's when the triplets—Mary, Martin, and Moses—come out the house. "Me too," they say, lining up like they in school, opening the door up wide and going back inside. Kee-lee's got seven brothers and sisters.

I wait for the triplets to come back out. They don't. I tell Kee-lee he better make them go to school. "Or your mother's gonna be mad."

"Who's gonna tell?"

I would never tell on Kee-lee, because he would never tell on me. And he knows stuff about me too. Like how on the day Jason died I ran to his place and cut my wrist with a knife. It was a little knife, but it drew blood. And one time I got so mad over Jason dying that I took rocks to the cocker spaniel in Mrs. Seymour's yard. Almost killed it. Only Kee-lee knows that. And he ain't telling.

Right when I get up to leave, Mary comes outside with a needle and thread. She hands 'em to Kee-lee, then sits in his lap, hugging him around the middle. He licks the thread. Sticks it through the needle hole. Knots it. Then sews up the square hole in the side of the shorts she handed him.

She jumps off his lap. "Thanks."

He smacks her butt, yelling after her, "Y'all don't make no mess in there."

Kee-lee's mom works in the factory way across town. She takes three buses and works double shifts sometimes. So even if he wanted, he couldn't get to school every day nohow. Some days he stays home with a sick kid or washes and irons their clothes for school the next day. His mom dropped out in the ninth grade. So did his grandmother and grandfather. So when Kee-lee says he's quitting, it's not that big a deal, I guess.

"Listen. I gotta go."

Kee-lee covers his mouth when he talks, so I don't think I really hear what I'm hearing when he tells me that they killed Moo Moo last night. Moo Moo is his cousin, and like a brother to me.

"He was sitting in his friend's ride, minding his own business." Kee-lee's got this funny look in his eye. "The guy next door told us first. He saw it on the eleven o'clock news."

Bang! The gun goes off in my head.

"I didn't hear about it," I tell him. "We don't watch the news no more."

Kee-lee and me say it at the same time. "We *is* the news."

It's a joke. Him and me used to say we were gonna be reporters. Take a camera through the neighborhood and show people what it's really like living here, being us. We were gonna call it *We Is the News—Life in the 'Hood*. But then we didn't have a camera. And anyhow, nobody would pay us for stuff they see every night on the TV for free.

"So I figure," Kee-lee says, "if I'm gonna die, why I gotta waste the time I do got sitting in school learning stuff I won't use?"

I need to get to school, but I don't move. I'm hoping Kee-lee's gonna say he was lying about Moo Moo. So I sit and remember how good he was to me. How him and me painted the porch up the block and made fifty bucks each. He would do stuff like that. Come and get me and Kee-lee. Take us on a job. Let us make some dough sweeping up or washing walls. He talked to me about my dad, too. He always said, "Mann. Give him time. It takes a while to get used to having a piece of you die."

I stand up. Walk down the steps and turn back Kee-lee's way. "Why'd he have to die?"

Moo Moo was twenty-eight. He wasn't all good, but he wasn't all bad neither. But around here, it don't matter. People get killed, good or bad, big or little.

Kee-lee's eyes tear up. I ask the question again, but I don't expect no answer. "Why . . . Why'd Moo Moo have to die?"

"That's just how it goes around here," Kee-lee says. "You get killed. Just 'cause."

 WALK UP THE street, past my house, heading for school. And even though I don't look at my front porch, I hear gunshots anyhow. *Bang!* Jason's gone. *Bang!* Kee-lee's cousin's gone. *Bang!* "You gonna be gone soon too," I say, turning around and heading back to Kee-lee's place.

Before I get to his house, my dad's first cousin stops me. He's a grown-up. His name is Semple, but we just call him Cousin. He lifts weights, so it's like he's always got his chest stuck out and his muscles tight. "Where you going, boy? School's that-a-way." He points.

I turn around. We stop in front of my house. I close my eyes because I know what's coming: a hug. A big long hug, like I'm some girl he likes. "Hey, Cousin," I say.

Cousin is always in a hurry. Talking and moving fast. Rushing even when he don't have to. He puts one foot on the steps and asks how my mom and dad are. I back up.

"Listen, Mann. The family . . ."

They say I look like Cousin, high yellow and gray-eyed. Only I'm short. Cousin's a big man with a big mouth. When he laughs, people turn around and look. When he talks, you wanna hold your ears. When you tell him a secret though, it stays secret. Like I told him about my dad being different since Jason died. And now Cousin comes by a couple times a month. "Just checking."

I stay a minute and tell him about Moo Moo. He's shaking his head, saying we're picking one another off faster than hard scabs. I don't know what that means. I don't care. "I gotta go to school," I lie.

He waves for me to come up the steps with him. I shake my head no. "Just this once," he says, ringing the doorbell. He tells me I won't ever get over Jason till I can walk on the porch. He pulls at the black bars, like he can rip 'em off with his bare hands. "Your father and these bars!" He shakes 'em. "This ain't no house! It's a prison! Before I'd live like this, I'd . . . I'd . . ."

My dad comes to the door and unlocks the iron gate. Cousin hugs him too. Then he gives him the book that's in his hand. "This the one?"

My dad walks past him and stands next to me on the pavement. "Yeah, this is it." He stares at the cover. There's two African boys holding spears on it. Then he gives me this *How come you ain't in school?* look, and I start walking.

The reason my father ain't full-out crazy is because of his family. They talk to him. Take us out, fix us food, and make sure we getting by okay. They always saying what Cousin says—move from around here. But we ain't got it as good as the rest. Most of them went to trade school or college. My dad went in the army and learned to fix tanks. Now he's a guard at a downtown store. "I'll move when I want to," he tells them. "Not because somebody's got a gun to my head."

My father tells me to get my butt to school, then they both go inside and lock the door behind them. I head for Kee-lee's.

Kee-lee is like me. He paints. He can take collard-green juice and make tree leaves or use tomato paste for blood.

"You do this?"

"Don't touch. It's wet."

He's got my front porch painted on his blue bedroom wall. Jason's there too. I turn away from the blood running out the side of his mouth. I check out Kee-lee's cousin instead. He's an angel. He's got on orange baggy jeans and see-through wings shaped like guitars. He's sitting on the roof of his car, looking over at Jason and pointing up to the sky.

Kee-lee opens a paint set as big as my desk in school. There's, like, thirty tubes of paint, chalk, charcoal, and a dozen brushes in it.

"Who stole it?"

He smiles. I figure it would be cool if he could paint his teeth white.

"I put it down my pants and walked out the store."

I wet a paintbrush. Dip it in Brown Bronze. Touch up Jason's skinny arms and legs. Dip the brush in paint and draw more charcoal-black naps on Moo Moo's head.

"I stayed up all night painting it."

The painting takes up half the wall. And it looks so real, I can't stop staring. Kee-lee's even got the Good Time bar that's up the street from us on the wall. There's trash on the ground and girls jumping rope, and Keisha braiding Kee-lee's hair. Right next to Jason's elementary school, there's a hoop game going on, with me, Kee-lee, Moo Moo, and Jason— all grown up. My eyes water. My fingers touch Jason's wet cheek. For a minute, I think about smearing his picture; wiping the whole wall clean. But even if I did, they'd still be dead. Still be gone for good. "You ever wanna hurt somebody, Kee-lee? Mess 'em up real bad?"

He smiles. His green teeth look gray.

"Ever get tired of doing what you supposed to do? Making everybody happy instead of you?"

He hands me a blunt. "You smoke, you no worry, Mann."

Kee-lee's been smoking up his allowance money ever since his boy Kelvin got killed last year walking out of school with his arm around somebody else's girl. Moo Moo stayed on his back about smoking weed. But he did it anyhow. It's gonna get worse now, I think.

I pick up another brush. "You know I don't smoke."

He finishes the rest, then gets down on the floor and starts eating sunflower seeds. "You need to smoke something, Mann. You can't stay regular in a house like yours. Too many crazy people. Too much drama."

I watch him shaking his leg like he does when he gets nervous or he's got something on his mind.

"Moo Moo shoulda—" I say.

Shells fly by my head. The trash can gets kicked over and next thing I know I'm pulling Kee-lee off me. "Shut up about Moo Moo! Shut up about dead people and dead stuff!"

I keep quiet, but not 'cause I'm scared. I'm thinking. Remembering. Wondering who gonna die next.

Chapter 5

**A**IN'T NO FUN playing hooky with a house full of little kids. So me and Kee-lee go to the horse stables. Dream-a-Lot Stables is twenty-eight blocks from my house, down in a valley. So even though it's not far from where I live, you don't just run into it. You gotta be looking for it. Otherwise, you'll never find it.

The owner asks how come we ain't in school, right when he's handing us a broom. For a one-hour ride, we gotta clean two stalls. When we done, we wet with sweat, and almost too tired to go riding. But it's been weeks since I rode Journey. So I get on her first. And soon as we're out the owner's sight, I smack her side, let the reins loose, and she takes off running.

Kee-lee's holding on to me. "Slow down."

I go faster, racing up the avenue between SUVs and hoopties. Passing boarded-up houses and burned-out stores. Forgetting about Jason and Moo Moo. Forgetting about the time somebody shot Journey too.

Kee-lee hollers in my ear. "Cops!"

I pull back on the reins and Journey slows up. The cop directing traffic eyeballs me. He knows we ain't allowed to have a horse in the streets. But where we live, people do things all the time they ain't supposed to. "Boy, shouldn't you be in school?"

Kee-lee answers. "That's where we headed, officer. This here horse is our show and tell."

The cop's whistle blows and his hand stops traffic. "Get down. Now."

Kee-lee smacks Journey's butt. Our light turns green. Cars fly up the street and so do we.

When our time's up, and Journey's back in her stall, we walk the neighborhood for a while, then take the bus over to Kee-lee's aunt's place. But as soon as she sees us, she's mad. And the next thing we know she's got us in the car and headed for school. She lies to the front-desk secretary. Says things got crazy at her place this morning with her husband's sugar acting up and the ambulance being called, and so, "These boys is late. Sorry."

I wish she hadn't done that, because not coming is better than coming in the middle of the day. See, when you don't show up, they call your house and say you didn't come and you can lie to your parents and say the teacher must've missed checking off your name. But when you don't come in on time and show up later, they call your house twice. Once to say you didn't show, next to say exactly what time you did come. Then you need a double lie, and those are hard to pull off. So when I get home, my father is waiting with the strap. I make up a lie; then a different one. Then two more. But he hits me with the belt anyway, and makes me tell the truth. Which gets me beat some more. I am too old to get beat. One time I almost hit my father back. But I remembered what Moo Moo said: "When somebody dies, it make you different, crazy inside." Moo Moo knew what was up, because his brother got shot dead in front of him ten years ago. It changed him. He started beating people up, stealing money, and smoking weed twenty-four/seven. "You get your right mind back, if folks give you time," he told me last year. "If they remember how sad you really is deep down inside."

My father is out of breath. He slaps his hand with the strap. "You learned your lesson, boy?"

I want to deck him. To beat him to the ground. Only Moo Moo woulda said, *Give him time, Mann.*

So that's what I do.

Chapter 6

HEN COUSIN knocked on our door at nine o'clock on a Saturday morning, my father got mad. We was all sleeping real good. "So?" Cousin said, when my dad let him in. "You can sleep anytime."

My mother walked by my room. She stopped, came inside and kissed me on the forehead. She asked me what I wanted to eat. Cousin yelled up the steps. He told her to come make him some banana pancakes and sausages. He said we'd better all get ready quick, because the family was coming in an hour to take us to the amusement park. I thought my dad would say he wasn't going. But he didn't. He ate two helpings of food and played chess with Cousin while my mother got dressed.

By the time my mom came back downstairs, the living room was full of people.

Aunts were sitting on chairs or leaning on walls eating French toast and bacon off paper plates, and telling kids to behave. My three uncles were standing up, watching basketball, drinking beer, and telling kids to stop blocking the TV. My mother was laughing. My father was showing off his new work boots. We were having a good time, just like regular people.

"Get over here, boy," my grandmother said, pulling me by the back of my pants.

I hugged her. "Yes, Ma Dear."

"You gonna ride with me? Go way up high in one of them rollie coasters?"

"You better not—"

Ma Dear told my father to mind his own business. "I'm your mother. And I'm seventy-four. I ought to know what I can handle."

Ma Dear and me always ride the roller coaster. Not the biggest ones, but the old wooden one that takes too long getting to the top, then only got two little hills on the way down. "I'll ride with you, Ma Dear."

She patted my hand. Asked me if I liked her fingernails. They're fake. "I ain't no old lady, you know." She stood up and headed for the kitchen. "You coming, child?"

I followed her. She stopped in front of Jason's room. I looked the other way. "No crying today." She took my hand and walked me into the kitchen. My mother was there, sitting by herself. Staring out the window. Ma Dear walked over to the yellow radio and turned it up loud. She clapped her hands and shook her big butt. "Dance with me." She moved side to side, singing with the music. "Grace. Can't you hear? Dance with me."

My mother couldn't help but laugh. My aunts and uncles stood in the doorway, shaking their heads and laughing too. "Shake it now."

I picked up my little cousin Ellen and swung her around. "Again," she said, leaning back and closing her eyes. "Faster."

My mother's head was bobbing. Her hands clapped, and next thing I knew somebody pushed my father into the kitchen and laughed when he started dancing like a man with two broken feet.

The whole house was shaking because people in the living room had the stereo on too. Little kids were jumping like somebody was turning rope. Grown-ups were doing the Slide and pushing furniture aside. Ma Dear was pulling out money, saying she was gonna pay two dollars to the best dancer. For a whole hour, all we did was act up, dance and sing, tell corny jokes, and talk about people's bald heads, bad feet, and beer bellies. I couldn't stop laughing. My father couldn't stop talking. And my mother was dancing so hard she was sweating out her hair.

Chapter 7

HEN MA DEAR and 'em come by, things round our house are good for a while. My father don't just go to work and come home mad. My mother stops crying and does the things she used to do—knit, visit the old woman up the street, cook, and sit on my bed and talk to me at night.

"What's shaking?" my father says, trying to be cool.

I'm in the basement, drawing. "Nothing."

He looks over my shoulder. Points to the charcoal drawing I'm making of Journey. She's not in her stall.

She's in an open field with ten other jet-black horses with fire-red eyes. Free. My dad sits down on the stool beside me. "Nice." He sets his coffee cup down. "Looks like the horses I used to have, except for the eyes."

My mom and dad are from Kentucky. His family lived on a farm. It wasn't theirs. It belonged to a white family. Ma Dear and them worked for the family, picking tobacco. My father was good with animals, so he got to ride the horses. He brushed them good and taught them stuff. "When I was your age," he says, touching Journey's tail, "I thought I would grow up and have a farm full of horses—dozens."

I put clouds in the sky. "Jason . . ."

My dad jumps up. "Wash up. Dinner's almost ready."

I forget sometimes not to say Jason's name. "I was just gonna say—"

My dad's halfway up the steps. "We had a good time, huh?"

Jason liked to draw, just like me. That's all I was gonna say.

My father bends over to tie his shoes. "At the park . . . last week."

I laugh. "Ma Dear better stay off them 'rollie coasters.' "

He backs down the steps. "The sign says, if you have a bad heart, don't get on." He sits down next to me. Tells me that every time she gets on a roller coaster he prays she'll make it off okay. Nobody will stop her from getting on, though, because she does what she likes. "Keeps her young," he says. "And strong."

I push my drawing in front of him. "Gonna get a A on this one."

"*Better* get an A. You been slipping since . . ." He doesn't finish saying what he's thinking.

I pack up my stuff. Change the subject. Try to keep things light. Then the phone rings. It's Kee-lee. He wants to come eat at our place. "To get away from all them bad kids."

My dad likes Kee-lee. When Jason was still alive, he took Kee-lee with us wherever we went. He taught all three of us to draw and ride horses. Now he don't hardly have nothing to do with Kee-lee. "I don't know."

"How come he can't never come over?"

He cracks his knuckles then breathes out loud. "Tell the boy to come. But don't be eating up all my food."

Dinner is just like that day we went to the amusement park. Everybody's laughing. Everybody's happy.

All Kee-lee does is make jokes, eat, and excuse himself when he goes to the bathroom to fart. "You got garlic in them potatoes, Ms. Grace. And garlic don't like me much."

When dinner's done, me and Kee-lee hang out in the basement. It's finished, with a new rug, video games, and a giant-size TV. Every now and then my father comes down and watches the game with us. He sits on the couch. Tells us why they need to trade number forty-five and number twenty-seven, then he goes back upstairs.

Kee-lee doesn't leave until the game ends at midnight. My father stands on the porch and watches him walk home. My mother sits on the couch next to me, saying she don't know the last time she made a meal that tasted so good. I'm sleepy. Tired. But I don't go to bed when they do. I stay up until three in the morning, painting. I don't paint nothing special, just me and my boy Kee-lee, standing on the corner playing hoops and talking trash.

Chapter 8

HEN SOMEBODY dies, do
you ever get him out of your head?

I wanted to ask my mother that. But her eyes were
extra red this morning, so I knew her and me was
both dreaming about Jason last night. And I couldn't
ask my father nothing like that, because he acts like
Jason was never born. So I just sit at the kitchen table
all by myself, eating hard grits and cold toast.

My father walks in after a while. "So where you
headed this morning?"

"School."

"To school is right. Skip out again and see what happens to you."

It's been a week since Kee-lee ate here, and things are just like always. Only I ain't the same. I skipped school again the other day. I went to Moo Moo's grave and had a good talk with him. Told him I was trying to hold on, to do right, but I keep having dreams about Jason, and getting headaches and feeling like being good ain't worth all the trouble. I mean, why should you go to school, get good grades, and listen to your parents when you gonna get shot anyhow? Why don't you just do like you wanna since you know you're gonna die before your time?

When my dad found out I cut, I told him where I went. Then I ducked. He ain't do nothing though. Just said I better not skip no more. And when I was almost out the room he said he was sorry for what happened to Moo Moo. That was the first time he said that.

Me and Kee-lee didn't go to the funeral they had for Moo Moo a couple of weeks back. We got dressed. We rode in the family car to the funeral. We lined up with the family and walked up the church steps. But right when we got to the door, and seen the silver casket all the way up front, him and me both stepped out of line at the same time. Kee-lee's mother looked mad. My dad grabbed me by the arm and said for me to come inside. But me and Kee-lee stayed put—right outside the church doors. In the rain. Waiting for it to all be over.

My mother walks in the kitchen and kisses me on the lips. "What color is sad?" she asks.

My father shakes his head and leaves the room. Since me and Jason was born, my mother always asked us nutty questions like that. "Black," I say.

She turns on the heat under the teapot and puts a mug on the table. "I think if sad were a color, it would be pink." She puts coffee in her cup and kisses me again before she sits down. "Or maybe it would be powder blue, like the sky on the prettiest day you ever seen."

My mom used to be a library aide, that's why she talks like that. But when Jason got shot, she couldn't work no more. All the quiet and all the kids just made her think about Jason too much.

The teakettle whistles. My mother tells me that sad has got to be a pretty color because pretty makes the heart hurt more than ugly does. "A smashed-up worm doesn't make you sad, but a round-eyed baby with a high fever do."

I think about all my paints. "Sad is yellow," I tell her, "like the sun first thing in the morning."

She puts sugar in her cup. "Like the sun," she says. "Like *my* son."

I let her know I gotta go, even though it's too early to leave for school. She says we'll all be better when Jason's birthday passes in six weeks. She looks at the funeral parlor calendar hanging on the wall over the sink. Today is May second. June twelfth is circled in red. A birthday sticker of cakes and candles covers the first day of this month. She puts one on every day, right up till his birthday. "That boy had me in labor sixteen hours. Then he came out long and red-faced with a head full of hair." She covers today's date with a pink cake.

I'm backing out the kitchen. Trying not to look at my mother, who used to be fat, and only weighs a hundred and ten pounds now. "Eat something."

"I'm not hungry," she says, like usual.

I walk over and hand her my hard toast. I break it in half, then in quarters. I put it to her lips. Her mouth won't open though. She starts talking about what kind of cake she's gonna make. Last year she made Jason's favorite—yellow cake with chocolate icing. This year she says she's making a pound cake and buying butter-pecan ice cream.

"I just want . . ." I keep my mouth shut. I unlock the doors and I leave, because I don't wanna say what I'm thinking—that I just want a regular mom, and I just want to be a regular kid who don't have to worry about ducking bullets or people dying around me like soldiers in a war.

Chapter 9

YOU CAN'T GO to school when your mother's in the kitchen baking a cake for your dead brother. So I go to Kee-lee's house. As soon as I get inside, I take a smoke from behind his ear and light up.

"When you start smoking?"

"Just now," I say, sucking in smoke. After it's half done, and I'm hot and dizzy, I put it out and take off my shirt. Kee-lee says that's how things go when you first start smoking. "Next time it won't be so bad."

We're up in his room with the dresser at the door to keep his brothers and sisters out. He's got

39

this here idea. Paint pictures of all the dead kids from our neighborhood. Put 'em on little cards and sell 'em.

"Let's not sell 'em," I tell him. "Just give 'em away."

Kee-lee's rolling up weed. Smoking it more and more now that Moo Moo's gone. Last week he lit up at school. The teacher almost busted him. "I ain't giving nothing away. I'm getting paid for my skills," he says, setting the bag of weed on the floor. "You know how many cats died around here this year?"

My stomach hurts.

"Twenty-five." He lights up. "I keep count, 'cause you never know," he says, taking a drag, "when you gonna be number twenty-six, or twenty-seven."

Nobody knows why, but for the last four years people been getting shot like crazy around here. It's not just gangs doing it. It's regular people too. Someone wants your ride and they shoot you for it. Somebody robs your mom, or was drinking with a friend and got mad 'cause his buddy tried to hit on his woman and he pulls out a gun. A lot of times kids get killed— even the cops seem to be gunning for us. It's like we're just in the wrong place at the wrong time; only all the time seems like the wrong time around here.

Kee-lee keeps telling me we can make some real

dough drawing pictures of Jason and them. "People can collect 'em like baseball cards."

I was thinking about Jason when I hit Kee-lee. Was thinking about him on a postcard with stuff on the back. *Jason Adler. Seven years old. First-grade student at Henry Ellen Elementary School. Played baseball. Liked to wrestle, play soldiers, and ride around the house on his father's back.*

Kee-lee touches the blood on his bottom lip, right before he swings a plastic baseball bat my way. "Hit me again and I'll smash your head in."

I tell him again that we ain't putting Jason on no cards. He's not listening. He wants to charge ten bucks apiece for the cards. And to start with Jason because he's little and people will feel so bad about him they'll want the others too.

He lights up a blunt and hands it to me. I take it this time, because my head won't stay off Jason, Moo Moo, my mother, and the cake. I suck smoke in and cough. Take another hit, and hold it in till my head spins. Next thing I know I'm lying on the floor, laughing. "Fruit trees." I take another puff. "Banana trees."

Kee-lee laughs. "What?"

"Killing round here would stop if we had more trees. "Apples trees. Pear trees . . . you know."

"What you talking about?"

"You ever hear of people getting shot on farms?"

"Huh?"

"You live on a farm around cows, and chickens, and trees, and ain't nobody gunning for you."

He laughs. "How 'bout trees with rice? I like rice."

"Rice don't grow on trees," I say. "It grows in water."

We laugh.

"No more weed for you," he says, walking over to the wall with Jason on it. He puts paint on a brush and touches up Jason's sneaker. "If he was my brother, I'd want him on a baseball card. I'd want everybody in the whole world to have his card, to not forget who he was."

I don't want Jason on no cards that people drop in the rain or use to light stoves when their pilot light goes out. Kee-lee still wants me to go along with it. But he knows better than to keep bugging me, so he changes the subject.

"California's got lots of fruit trees and people get shot there."

I think on that awhile. "Do they get shot on farms too, Kee-lee?"

He says he don't know. "I ain't never been on no farm." He spits sunflower-seed shells on the floor. "Maybe it's just the chickens that get shot. And the cows."

I sit straight up. "Who's gonna shoot a cow? They don't do nothing bad."

Kee-lee don't answer for a while. "Who's gonna shoot a little boy?" he says. "They don't do nothing bad neither."

Chapter 10

T WAS KEE-LEE'S idea. Sneak out tonight and get Moo Moo's car. Ride it around town. Come daylight, take it to the park and wash it. That way Moo Moo would know we ain't forget about him.

Moo Moo always kept his keys in the glove compartment. And he never locked his ride. So when we get to his car at two o'clock in the morning, it's sitting there just like always—unlocked, waiting to hit the streets again.

Kee-lee's mom's got more sisters than I got

fingers. Most of 'em live around our way so we ain't have to go far to get to his Aunt Jessie's place. Soon as we there, we see the tree they planted in Moo Moo's name. It's skinny, but there's plenty of white flowers covering it. And right at the roots, there's a bronze plaque with a picture of Moo Moo sketched on it. He's got his arms folded and one foot on his car fender. Kee-lee did the picture. It looks just like him.

I'm reading the plaque. Kee-lee's in the car, gassing the engine. Moo Moo woulda been mad at him for doing that. "Shirlee's my sweet thang," he used to say. "Can't be rushing her, getting her all hot and bothered."

Kee-lee guns the engine again. I open the passenger door and tell him to quiet down. He smoked a little something on the way over, so he ain't in his right mind. "I'm doing this for my cuz," he says, too loud for this time of night.

"Shhh."

He puts the car in park, steps out and shouts, "Moo Moo!"

"Get back in, Kee-lee."

He slaps his chest. "Moo Moo!"

The upstairs light in the house comes on.

"I ain't forget about you, man!" He lays his face on the roof of the car. For a minute, I think he's gonna cry. "Never gonna forget you, bro."

The window goes up. "Who that?" A woman in a purple scarf's got her head stuck out the second-floor window. It's Aunt Jessie, Moo Moo's mom.

We get in the car.

"Get out! That's my baby's car!"

The car's backing up and headed for the tree. "Turn! Turn the wheel!"

Kee-lee can't drive. He's only been behind the wheel a few times when Moo Moo was giving us lessons. The car jumps off the curb. The back wheels are in the street, and the front wheels are in the grass, kicking up dirt. Kee-lee shifts gears without putting on the brakes. My chest bangs into the dashboard. He puts the car in reverse, right when his aunt runs up to the car and points to him through the window. "Kee-lee. I'm gonna kill you, boy!"

He guns the engine. Black smoke comes out the tailpipe. The car flies across the street backward, heading for a blue SUV. Kee-lee stops the car cold, and him and me almost go out the back window. His aunt's following us, saying for him to get out the car. I'm staring out the other window, hoping she don't recognize me. Kee-lee shifts gears. His aunt curses. I hold on to the seat. The car jerks forward; speeds backward. Stops. Kee-lee shifts gears again, driving up the street with his aunt banging on the trunk, running behind us, begging us to stop.

When we get to the park, Kee-lee gets out from behind the wheel, shaking. I'm thinking it's because all the driving made him nervous. But he says it's because he's still high. "And my hands won't do what my head tells 'em to." We step out the car and sit in the dark under a broken streetlight. "You lucky you ain't dead, Mann."

"It was fun," I tell him.

He's lying on the ground, looking like he's gonna be sick. "I ain't doing that no more."

I lean on Moo Moo's ride and wonder what he's doing right now.

Kee-lee and me remember a lot of things about Moo Moo. Like the time we played football with him and his college friends. Or the time he took us to some girl's place and her friends kissed us on the lips and let us see their underwear drawer. It was never nothing big that Moo Moo did with us. It was a lotta small things; nothing that cost money or took up too much time. It was just being round Moo Moo. Him rubbing my head and telling me I needed a haircut. Him dropping by school and driving us home. Or him sitting by me at Jason's funeral saying, "You still got a brother, Mann. Me."

Kee-lee interrupts my thoughts. "Who's gonna look out for me, Mann?"

I don't move when Kee-lee says that. 'Cause I don't have no answer for him.

"I mean, your father dropped me after Jason passed. But Moo Moo, he was always around. Always checking in on my mom and us; driving past the house and . . . well."

Kee-lee's standing up and patting himself down, feeling around for a blunt. Pulling out a match. Striking it. I watch his fingers shake in the night. "He was my godfather."

"I know."

"We ain't tell too many people. Didn't want them to think we was punks."

"I know."

Smoke blows my way.

"They shoulda shot me instead of him."

I don't move. Not one muscle.

"I mean . . . they shoulda just shot me dead and

got it over with, instead of taking people from me one by one."

Kee-lee don't have to explain nothing to me. I know what he's talking about. It ain't just his boys that keep getting killed; his daddy took a bullet too. That was long ago, when Kee-lee was seven; two years after his dad moved out.

Kee-lee walks over to me and slams his fist into my chest. "What you gonna do? Cry?" He jumps back, toting that blunt, his eyes closed and his head rocking side to side. "Don't do no crying out here, you baby, sissy girl," he says, sounding like my father. "You do, and you gonna get hurt."

I throw a punch. He ducks. He aims for my head and misses. We boxing and talking about Moo Moo, how he taught us to fight. We laughing about the time he let us watch him make the moves on some girl. Kee-lee hands me the blunt. I take it. Smoke it. I'm glad when it clouds up my head and makes me forget about all the bad stuff that's come my way lately. In a little while, everything's okay. Kee-lee's happy. I'm happy. And having Jason and Moo Moo gone don't make us all that sad, for now anyhow.

I go to the trunk for the buckets and lamb's-wool rags Moo Moo always kept there, and we walk over to the water spigot, fill up the bucket and head back to the car. We take our time washing Shirlee's tires and hood, rubbing dust off her doors and dirt from underneath her belly. Then we rub her dry. Wax her till she shines. And when he thinks I ain't watching, I see Kee-lee kiss her, right where Moo Moo always did— on the hood of the car, right on the driver's side.

Chapter 11

Y FATHER found out about us stealing Moo Moo's car. He made me stand in the corner for two hours with one leg up. My mother got mad at him. Said he was being ridiculous and she wasn't gonna put up with him being cruel to me. They argued about it for a long time. He did what she said, though, and let me go to my room. They agreed that I wouldn't be allowed to watch TV or go over Kee-lee's place for a month. But when she went to the store after supper, he took me on a little ride.

Kee-lee asks me sometimes why I don't just clock

my dad and get it over with. It's coming, too. I know it. So I let my dad slide. Give him more rope than I should—for now.

My dad's truck is packed with shovels, trash bags, and brooms. He don't explain why he's got all those things. But when we get to the corner of Seymour and Lincoln, I know why. There's an empty lot there where people dump garbage and trash, couches and dead cats, bricks and bottles too.

He opens his door. Walks around and opens mine. "All right," he says. "Get out. Get busy."

I look at the lot. I look at him. "No."

This ain't no little lot. A four-story house used to be on it. And people do all kinds of things in it. Shoot up. Throw up. Pee it up. Junk it up. There's rats in there. Cockroaches too, I bet.

Ain't no expression on my dad's face, so you can't tell if he's sad, glad, or mad. "You think you a man, huh?" He pulls my arm. My feet spread and press to the floor like I'm on a roller coaster headed down. I wrap my arms around the back of my seat. He yanks me by the arms like the chain on a stopper in a drain. I fly out my seat. Fall out the car. Stare up at him from the ground. Then I jump up swinging.

A punch heads for my stomach—but it don't land

on me. Fists go to my head, my chest, and my face, but they all pass by me. That pisses me off, 'cause I know what my dad is trying to say: *Anytime I want, I can take you outta here.*

He looks at me. "Pick a spot. Any spot."

I got one picked out right on the side of his mouth where his bad tooth acts up sometimes. "Don't think I won't hit you." I swing and miss. Back up. Bounce on my toes like he taught me. I bob, swing, and hit him in the side of his head as hard as I can. "Yeah!"

A left hook, and I'm down on the ground and can't get up. A few minutes later, I'm doing what he told me in the first place, and he's headed for the truck. "Dopeheads live in this kind of filth all the time," he says, throwing a box of trash bags at my head. "You wanna do dope, might as well start now living like they do."

I look at him and try to figure out how he knows I been smoking weed. He gets in the jeep. Tells me to stop being soft and clean up the lot. "Otherwise you gonna be here all night long."

My dad is super hard on me because he thinks he was too soft on me and Jason before. He says that most boys in our neighborhood are used to life being hard. When trouble comes, they knock it out the way. "Or at least run from it." Jason just stood there—wetting himself. "Too many hugs," my father says now. "Not enough butt-kickings." My mother says that ain't so. My father disagrees. "The hard knots don't die. They kill and survive. The ones that have been hugged and kissed and loved too much—they being picked off like cotton from a pod. They soft. Momma's boys," he says. "And ain't no more momma's boys coming out *my* house."

People watch. They shake their heads and say it's a shame what my father's doing. But nobody calls the police or gives me a drink or says for him to stop. And four hours later—after I worked two whole hours in the dark—my dad says I can quit. There's ten garbage bags on the ground. "Load 'em," he says, sitting in the truck, eating chips, and holding on to the book Cousin gave him.

I pick up the bags and dump them into the back of the truck. My dad says I stink, so he don't let me ride up front. I'm sitting in back with the trash, holding on tight with one hand, dropping bags in the street with the other. When we get to the dump, I unload the rest of the bags. My father listens to the radio. When we get home, I'm too tired to climb out the truck.

He hollers. My mother cries. I can't move. And finally, my father helps me in the house. "Boy," he says, pulling my dirty shirt over my head when we get upstairs, taking down my pants, and throwing my underwear in the trash. He walks me to the shower and stands me under the warm water. "Boy," he whispers in my ear, "I can't lose no more . . ."

The water stings like alcohol when it hits the cuts on my fingers and legs. I open my mouth and drink it down like warm tea.

My dad squeezes soap over my shoulders and cleans under my nails. "Boy, I can't bury no more sons."

Chapter 12

SMELL NOW THAT I don't go to school. I stink, really. My mother asks how come that is. "You shower every morning. I hear the water."

I go in and sit down on the john and smoke weed out the window. But I don't shower.

"Comb your hair," she says, picking lint out my 'fro. "That's the style? Well, I don't like it." She hands me her deodorant and says to put some on in front of her so she can see me do it. "You're changing out them clothes. Right in front of me." She sits at the kitchen table and tells me to slow down. "Stuffing food in your mouth like you haven't eaten in months, when late last night you ate everything in sight."

My mother and me sit and talk for a while. I'm high, but I can still tell she's having a good day. She's wearing her favorite dress—the light green one with the pink flowers. And she's got her hair fixed nice, and lipstick on too. "You look pretty."

She spoons eggs into my mouth. "The closer we get to Jason's birthday, the worse things get here." She wipes my mouth with her napkin. "But I can't let the whole house fall apart." She breaks off bacon and sticks it in my mouth. "I gotta get back to who I was before: a good mother, a good wife."

My father walks into the room with his uniform on. He's just a security guard—nobody important—but he walks so straight and tall, and his clothes are so neat and pressed, you'd think he was leaving home to run the world or something. "How come your eyes are red?"

I lie. "I ain't sleep good."

He sniffs my shirt. "You been smoking weed again? In my house?"

My mother leans over and smells me too. She tells my dad that they have to do something about me. He says he tried two weeks ago when he made me clean up the lot. "You called it abuse. Happy now?"

She walks over to the stove and cracks six eggs in a hot pan. "It was abuse." She comes over to me and rubs my cheek. "He should be back in therapy. I'll call somebody today. Anybody." Her lips kiss my cheek. "We need help."

When the eggs are done, she goes and puts a cake sticker on the calendar. Jason's birthday is in two weeks. She rubs the shiny paper like it's his face she's touching.

My dad sits down. He says that our neighbor, Miss Lucille, saw me talking with Ace. He sells weed. Killed a few people too.

I jump up out my seat. "I wasn't with no Ace!" I reach across the table and get more bacon. "Can't I just eat without y'all bothering me?" I grab four pieces of bacon, stick 'em in between a buttered biscuit, and shove half the sandwich in my mouth. Butter drips down my lips like blood.

My father pulls me up from the table by my collar. Biscuit mixed with bacon falls out my mouth and onto the kitchen table. "I told you if I ever found out you was smoking in my house . . ."

I laugh. I don't mean to, but I do.

My mother acts like she's just figuring everything out. "That boy's high."

My father pulls off his thick black belt and starts whupping me. My mother don't stop him. She covers her mouth and bites down on her fingers like she's watching a scary movie.

When you getting beat, you gotta keep moving. So I'm running in circles. Jumping up and down. Ducking when the black strap swings at my head. Laughing because he's hitting hisself right along with me. Then the belt buckle hits me in the lip. And while my father is apologizing to my mother, and I am holding my busted lip, I say, "That ain't hurt."

My mother tells me to keep my big mouth shut. I don't know why I keep talking, but I do. I tell my dad I'm calling Child Welfare. I sit down in the chair. Put my feet on the table and pick up that book he's always reading now. "What kind of mess you reading?"

Right then my dad tackles me. He knocks me to the floor. Drags me by one arm through the living and dining rooms and over to the front door. He opens it wide. Picks me up by my shirt and pants and throws me onto the front porch.

Weed makes you do stuff you shouldn't do, like get your dad so mad he don't care no more that you're scared to touch the porch with your baby finger, let alone put your whole body on it.

Soon as I hit the floor, I stop breathing. All the air in me dries up like the blood on our porch. "I can't . . . breathe." I'm pulling at the skin on my neck, trying to get air.

My mother holds me. Whispers in my ear for me to calm down. "You're all right. Just calm down. Just . . ." She stares at my dad. "Get him up." She rubs my chest. "Mann. The blood's all gone." She's talking to my dad again. "You don't get my boy off this here porch right now, I'm gonna carry him off myself, and when I'm done, I'm coming back for you."

Air sneaks into my lungs. I take a long, deep breath, coughing hard and trying to get up. My father and mother carry me. "It's okay," they say, together. "You'll be okay."

Mann!

I turn to see who's calling me.

Play soldiers with me.

My hands and feet get ice-cold. "Jason?"

My father looks around. My mother does too.

Catch me. Okay?

I ask my parents if they hear Jason. If they see him.

My dad looks at me. "See what happens when you smoke that dope?"

I close my eyes tight. But I still see blood. And I still hear him laughing, just like that day when he got shot. *Mann*, he said, when I went for the hose. *What you get when you cross a pickle with a pencil?*

Little-kid jokes ain't never funny. So I told him I didn't know, didn't care. Then he walked over to the steps and sat down. *You get*, he said, laughing real hard like it was gonna be a really funny joke. *You get . . .*

I didn't hear the answer, because Journey was thirsty. She needed a drink. So I left Jason all by hisself. And that's how come he got killed.

Chapter 13

OR TWO WHOLE weeks, I didn't go over to Kee-lee's house. I didn't smoke no weed or cut class. And when Jason's birthday came, I didn't even cry when my mother blew out the candles and my father told him he was always gonna be his son. I left right after the cake and ice cream and went to the stables to see Journey.

The sign on the gate said the stables were closed until further notice. I climbed over the busted wooden fence anyhow. Walked through the chewed-up grass and hard dry dirt and down the long dirt path. I opened the stable door and got real sad when I saw her. She was skinnier than usual, and her eyes looked sad, like my mother's. "He took off and left you, huh, girl?" I didn't try not to step in her mess, 'cause mess was everywhere. So I kept walking—feeling poop squeeze up in the hole in the bottom of my sneaker and stick to the bottom of my pant legs like glue. I took carrots out my pocket and fed them to her. "Hungry?" I patted her face and fanned flies and gnats away.

Journey was so hungry she bit my hand trying to eat the carrots. So I opened my backpack and took out more food—lettuce, corn on the cob, and zucchini. "You can't carry me nowhere today, huh?" I said, tickling her chin. Telling Journey her teeth are whiter than Kee-lee's, then going for the water hose to give her a drink. "Jason's birthday's today," I said, pressing my finger over the hose and making Journey a fountain. "You remember Jason, right?"

Journey moved her head. She remembered. I knew it. I dropped the hose. Held her face between my hands and stared into her eyes. "You still see what they done to him?" She tried to pull free. "I do." She neighed, just like she did that day at our house. "I see him all the time. Dead. Him and Moo Moo dead and gone."

Journey yanked her face away. Her big lips pulled back over her yellow teeth and wiggled back and forth like she was trying to talk to me.

"Okay, girl," I said, picking up the broom and shovel. "Let's clean your stall and get you some more food."

Journey is like me: just regular. Nothing special. But she stands tall with her head up, like she's one of them horses the Queen of England rides sometimes. Only today, standing tall don't help her none, because you can still see her ribs, still not forget that she ain't nothing but a five-buck-an-hour riding horse.

I slap my thigh. "Give me your foot." I lift her foot. Scrape doo-doo and dry grass out from under her broken shoes with a hoof pick. I ask if she remembers the time Jason bit her. "I wanna see if she tastes like chicken," he told my dad. He was three. We came to the stables once a week to ride then. My father figured five bucks an hour was a good deal, even for a horse with fleas. But when he started bringing us two and three times a week, my mother complained about the money. That's when my father struck a deal with Mr. Zingerfeld, the owner, that we'd clean the stalls, keep Journey brushed and fed, and ride her as much as we wanted.

After I got done cleaning Journey's shoes and cleaning her stall, I went to check on the other horses. One horse got worms, I seen 'em in his stools. And his black coat was eaten away in some places. I gave him a drink and the last of the hay. He lay in the corner, too tired or hungry to stand. I sat down next to him in all that stink, and rubbed him. He lay his head in my lap. "Why everything around here die?" I asked. Then I got up and took a shovel and cleared the mess away.

The third horse, Maiden Lucy, was the strongest. So I opened her stall and watched her run for the grass. She snatched it out the ground, swallowed it, then ate till she pooped.

It was dark when I got home. I came in the back way, leaving my clothes and shoes in the basement. I showered and put on my pajama bottoms. My mother was in bed asleep. My father was sitting in the living room with the lights off, with a bottle of Scotch and no glass. I thought he'd be mad at me for being gone all day long. He wasn't. "I figured this once," he said, "you had a right to take off."

Him and me sat there, not talking, but listening just the same. Me, I was listening for Jason, because when I walked in the house I thought I heard him say,

What you get me for my birthday? I pulled out a little green soldier from my pocket. It had been sitting on the washing machine this morning, right next to Jason's favorite red shorts. I said good night to my dad, went to my room, and locked the door. I opened my drawer and took out the picture I had drawn late the night before when my mother wouldn't stop crying. "Happy birthday, Jason," I said, staring at a picture of him sitting on Journey, riding back home with a grin on his face.

Chapter 14

IRST THING the next morning, I told my father about what I seen at the stables. He called the police. They said they would go over there right away. "If I had money, I'd buy that place," he said. "Always wanted to own a horse. Always wanted to teach boys to ride and respect living things."

My dad said that on Tuesday. The County found a safe place for the horses to live by Friday, and another kid got shot round our way on Saturday. She was sitting in a car talking to a friend. A jet-black coupe pulled up. The window rolled down. Bullets went everywhere. I ain't see it for myself, but it was all over the TV. The girl who died was sixteen—ready to graduate school and go down south to college. She won a full scholarship to Spelman and was gonna work in the mayor's office for the summer. So when she got buried, seems like everybody in the whole city came to her funeral. The picture in the newspaper was real sad. But I didn't cry. You can't cry for everybody who gets shot—otherwise you'd cry your life away.

Today's the day after that girl's funeral and my dad just said he was sending my mother away.

"What?"

He pours milk in my glass then puts the carton down before the glass is full. "Pour your own milk."

I pick up the carton of chocolate milk and drink out of it. He shakes his head. He says my mother needs a rest. I think she's just getting on his nerves. Since he threw me on the porch, she's been on his case. Telling him to watch how he talks to me. Sitting down with him at night and trying to get him to talk about Jason.

"Where's she going?"

"Kentucky."

I wipe milk off my mouth. "Why she gotta go?"

He looks at me like I'm nuts and says she has to

go so she can stop making cakes, remaking Jason's bed, and being sad all the time.

I do not want to stay home alone with my dad. But he says my mother always comes back from Kentucky feeling better about things. He thinks if we let her know it's okay to go, she'll feel better about leaving. "And come back like her old self."

He packs tuna sandwiches and doughnuts in the red cooler, and unlocks the kitchen door. "Anyhow, while she's gone, I'm gonna teach you some stuff."

"What kinda stuff?'

"Stuff women can't teach boys."

I rub my chin. "Like how to get a girl to—"

When my father yells at you, it makes you feel like a dog that just messed the living-room rug. "There's more to being a man than just getting into some girl's pants!"

I stare at the floor. "Sorry."

He slams the door. I look up. Twenty minutes to go before school starts, I think. I call Kee-lee to see if he has some weed.

"Always," he says.

I sit up on the kitchen counter.

"A penny for your thoughts," my mother says, right when I'm hanging up the phone.

I want to tell her not to go to Kentucky. Then I hear my dad say in my head, *Be a man. Not no baby sissy girl who needs his momma to wipe milk off his chin.* So I keep my mouth shut. My mother opens the door wide and the sun comes through the bars and makes thick black lines on the floor. She's singing. Whistling. Opening and closing kitchen cabinet doors and pulling out a box of noodles, tomato sauce, and Italian seasoning. "Gonna make lasagna for tonight." She sits ground beef on the table. "Your dad's favorite."

My mother used to sing all the time. Not no church songs neither. Songs from the sixties and seventies. "Your father tell you I'm taking a trip?"

"Yeah."

She cuts the fire up under the frying pan and dumps bloody red hamburger meat in it. "He thinks I'm going to get away from Jason's memory." The ground beef turns gray and pieces of the meat wiggle in the pan like worms on a hot car. "But I'm going to find us a new place to live."

I jump to the floor. "I ain't living in the country."

She scrambles the meat. "Rather die here?"

Before I can answer, she's singing, " 'Sugar Pie, honey bunch. You know that I love you.' "

"Remember that song?" she says, shaking her hips. "'I can't help myself . . .'"

She dances over to me, holding the white plastic spatula in the air. Letting hamburger juice drip down her arm and onto the floor she made me scrub two nights ago. "'I love you and nobody else,'" she says, taking my arm.

I don't wanna dance with my mother. But she's happy and singing and glad for the first time in a long while so I let her hold my hands. Let her dip me, and turn me in circles, and tell me stupid jokes that Jason used to tell us all the time.

"They're not taking any more boys from me. No, sir," she says, squeezing me to her. "I'm going south. Gonna stay as long as I need to. And when I come back," she turns my fingers loose and runs to the burning pan, "we're gonna have a new place to live. A nice safe place where the stink of death ain't in your nose all the time." She sneezes and pinches her nose and wipes her hands on her apron. "Don't tell your father nothing I said, hear?"

Pouring garlic powder in the meat, stirring in dried onions, she tells me about our land in Kentucky—fifteen acres she had since she was ten. My father doesn't know she owns it. It was her secret stash, she says. Something for me and Jason when we were grown. She gives me this look, like she can see me never growing old. "I will take you from him—from here."

She reaches for the ketchup. "Your dad doesn't see what he's doing to you." She sings while she squeezes. "But I do. And I'm gonna stop him. I have to."

Chapter 15

Y FATHER'S people came by today. They don't ever say they coming, they just show up—"Like rain," my dad says. I like that. Not knowing and being surprised. My dad doesn't always go for it, though. When they showed up, he started cussing. Saying he wished they would just leave us alone. My mother was glad though. "I get tired," she said, "of being sad."

Soon as they stepped foot in the house, the music went on. The bass made the glasses shake.

My father yelled, "Cut that down!"

Ma Dear called him a grouch. She took out the playing cards. Aunt Sassy went to the basement and brought up the card table, and Cousin lit up the grill on the front porch. "After this," Ma Dear said, "we're going to the mall. There's a new movie out."

My father sat down next to her. Ma Dear covered his hand with hers. "Tell me a good joke."

He said he didn't know any.

She watched Aunt Sassy wipe the table off. "I figured you'd say that, so I got one of my own." Ma Dear dealt cards to my mother and father, Aunt Sassy, Cousin, his girlfriend, and me. "What do you get when you cross a man with a chicken?"

Cousin laughed. "A man who can lay eggs?"

I took a guess. So did my mother. Ma Dear said we were all wrong. When we asked her what you get when you cross them, she said she didn't know. "Don't remember. I'm seventy-four, you know. Can't be expected to remember every itty-bitty thing."

I looked at Cousin's girlfriend, Itah. She looked at my dad. My mother looked at her bare feet and we all started laughing at the same time. I told Ma Dear she don't ever need to tell a joke. "Because you always mess them up."

She pinched my nose. "But I still know how to make y'all laugh, don't I?"

We laughed when Cousin Semple burned the hot dogs. Laughed some more when Ma Dear and Cousin's girlfriend started arguing. "Your dress is too short," Ma Dear told her. "Don't get mad at me for saying what everyone's thinking." We laughed when my father took a nap on the couch and my little cousin put orange lip gloss on his lips and painted his fingernails pink.

When Ma Dear and them come, it's like some-body breathing air into a person who almost drowned. The whole house comes alive. Curtains blow when there ain't even no wind. The sun shines off water glasses and warms up cold tea. People sing and dance and pee themselves for laughing so hard. It ain't right, I think sometimes, that the good times leave when they do. So when everybody's still laughing and drinking and having fun, I sneak up to my room and come down with charcoal and my drawing pad.

"It's a gift," Cousin says, standing over me.

My father says it's not a gift. "It's a present, from me. I taught him to paint, you know."

Itah pulls at her skirt. "Them hands gonna make you famous one day. Watch and see."

I tell them to go away. I can't draw if everybody's behind me. Ma Dear says it's kitchen time. That means everybody's gotta grab something, wash something, and put away something. I stay put. Draw the little ones walking like ants into the kitchen with ketchup and mustard and beans. Draw Ma Dear with my dad's arms around her, tying her apron. And I put my mother in the kitchen laughing, even though she's really by Jason's bedroom door looking sad.

"That's for me, right?" Ma Dear says, coming into the living room with wet hands. "Gonna frame it and put it up over my couch."

Ma Dear's living room is full of family pictures and drawings by me. "You can have it."

She leans over and sticks her cheek out for a kiss. "You ain't spent the night since Jason passed. Time you did that, don't you think?"

I don't spend the night nowhere no more. My mother would worry if I did.

Ma Dear knows that. "She don't blame you. Nobody blames you."

I look at my dad. She takes my hand and we go into the kitchen. "He don't blame you either." She takes off her apron and opens the oven to check on the pineapple upside-down cake she's making. "You know you can always come and live with me, if the road's too hard here."

I stick my fingers in the icing for the blueberry muffins she made earlier. "I'm all right."

She sits the hot pan on the counter. Takes a knife and cuts me a big slice of cake. "One day everything's gonna be regular again."

How's it gonna be regular, I think, if Jason's never coming home?

Chapter 16

HEY KEEP KILLING people for no real reason. A boy walks out his house and goes to the store for milk and *Bang!* He's dead. A little girl, Jason's age, is jumping double Dutch on her front porch and *Bang!* She's gone too. The grown-ups do what they always do; nothing. Last week the preachers held hands with the politicians and walked around the corner seven times. Nothing changed. Two people was still dead. Everybody else is just plain scared.

We talk about the killings in history class. Our teacher says they're random: done for no real reason.

I raise my hand. I tell her that when I was little, I would bury pennies in the dirt. Ain't have no real reason. I just did it because I could, I guess. "Good analogy," she says.

Then Rock, a kid sitting across the room from me, says maybe some of the dead people got what they deserved. "People do stuff," he says, standing up even though the teacher ain't tell him to. "They step on your new sneakers or touch your four-hundred dollar jacket." He's rubbing his arm like he can feel the leather.

Mrs. Seigner says he's being ridiculous.

"Naw. Naw!" he says, jumping around. "You be riding in a car and they cut you off." He punches his hand. "Somebody might have to die for that one."

Cheryl Keller don't raise her hand. She just starts talking. "Little kids been getting killed too."

"So?" Rock says. Everybody stares at me. "They mighta did something." He smiles. "You know how bad little kids is these days."

My little brother Jason had a hundred little green soldiers. Every day he sat on the porch and played with them. That's what he was doing when the bullets found him.

Mrs. Seigner keeps cutting her big blue eyes at me.

"Sit down," she tells Rock. But he's got more to say.

"Mrs. Seigner, you don't know, because you don't live around here. Everybody's got guns." He crosses his arms and leans against the wall. "And everybody knows they gonna die young."

Mrs. Seigner is white, with long blond hair and too much jewelry for a neighborhood like this. She stops, and the big gold cross around her neck keeps moving. "That's ridiculous." She goes to the front of the class and tells us to take out our notebooks.

Rock ignores her. "I'm just saying, what it matter if you die at seventeen or seven? You dead regardless."

I ain't notice I was rocking till I hit my spine on the back of my seat. Ain't notice I was cracking my fingers and stomping my right foot on the floor neither.

Mrs. Seigner looks back at me. "Mann, are you all right?"

"Yeah."

"Okay, class. Let's change the subject."

"Seven-year-olds can't do nothing to make you kill them," I say.

She tells us again to drop the subject.

I'm walking over to Rock, knocking on every desk I pass. I push him. "Tell me. What a little boy do to get shot?"

Rock jumps up and pushes me back. Good, because now I got a reason to knock his head off.

The teacher steps in between us. "Break it up."

"Maybe your brother wouldn't shut up or something. Like you," Rock says, pushing so I stumble.

I pick up Britney Allen's history book, but the teacher takes it from me. Rock's on his tiptoes, reaching past her, trying to get to me. "After class," he says, knowing full well he's gonna try to take me soon as he can.

Everybody's on their feet. Saying who they think's gonna win the fight.

I go to my seat. Let him know I'm ready for him. When everybody's seated, and Mrs. Seigner's at the blackboard, Rock tells the boy next to him, "He probably got his own brother shot with that big mouth of his."

Mrs. Seigner shoulda moved when I asked. That way I wouldn'a had to knock her down. But I wasn't gonna let him say nothing like that. So I wasn't sorry when I took my boot and kicked him in the leg till I heard something crack. Wasn't sorry one little bit for busting his lip, biting his finger till it turned deep purple, and knocking out three of his teeth.

The guards at school tried to catch me. But I am faster than any kid at school, so I can outrun two fat guards with uniforms so tight their pants fit like sausage skins.

My father's home when I get there. And as soon as he sees me he knows something's wrong. Not just because of how I look, but because I walk in through the front door.

"They gonna lock me up." I try to catch my breath. "For killing somebody."

My mother walks out of the kitchen. "Oh my God!"

My father is heading for his desk drawer. Pulling out his gun. Loading it. "Who's gonna kill you?" He pulls the string and the blinds shut. He locks the front door and tells me and Momma to get down on the floor.

My mother is screaming, saying she can't lose another son. I'm trying to tell them what happened. But they ain't listening. They peeking out the window for somebody who ain't even coming.

"Listen!" I sit down on the couch. "Listen to me." I tell them what I did.

My mother's hand covers her mouth the whole time. My father's gun lies in his lap. "Let's go," he says, standing up.

"Where?"

He goes to his desk. Puts the gun in the drawer. Locks it. And rubs his head and cheeks with his fingertips. "To school. To the police."

I'm waiting for him to hit me. To yell or maybe take the gun or knife out and use it on me. But he walks into the kitchen, dips a dry towel in the boiling water my mother's got on for coffee, and washes blood off my fingers, from around my lips and neck. "Get him a new shirt. Some pants, too."

My mother walks up the steps, shaking her head. My dad pats me on the back. "You got him 'fore he got you, Mann. Good."

I'm thinking he's trying to trick me or something. So I apologize for what I did.

"You ain't in trouble with me," he says, reaching in his pants pocket and pulling out a twenty. "That's the kind of boy that'll shoot you dead if he gets the chance. So you gotta set 'em straight first. Let 'em know you a man, not some boy people can push around."

My mother hears what he says. Walking back down, she asks if he's lost his mind. He says he wishes he'd taught Jason to use his fists. "Or a gun even."

She screams. "Fists don't stop bullets! And guns

don't stop trouble from landing on your front porch!"
She pulls me over to her. Whispers in my ear. "One
day we gonna live where people don't fight and shoot
so much."

My father pulls me over to him. "Boy. I'm gonna
teach you some things you gonna need to know to
stay safe around here."

My mother twists my left arm. "You in trouble
right now for—"

"You don't know if he's gonna be in trouble," my
dad says, "if it's self-defense."

"He thinks he bit somebody's finger off! That's
self-defense?" She gets up in my father's face.
"That's what a man's supposed to do? Hurt other
men? Other boys?"

My dad tells my mother to keep quiet and let
him handle things. Then he puts his arm around my
shoulder, and we walk out the front door. Together.

Chapter 17

HEY KICKED ME out of school. Said I can't ever come to a public school in this city again because I'm too violent. They put me in juvey for four weeks—till my trial came. But the judge let me out on probation. He read the psychologist's report. "Mann is a smart, nonviolent youth who suffers from severe depression as a result of his brother's murder," it said. "Confinement would make matters worse. Advise weekly, long-term counseling."

It wasn't right for me to hurt somebody, but it's like hurting Rock changed things for me. It got me to talking about things. Like how I feel it's my fault Jason got killed. And why I can't sleep through the night like regular people. It got my parents talking too.

For a while, we was all different. My dad went around the house whistling. And he made it so me being stuck in the house—just in case Rock wanted revenge—wasn't so bad. Every day after work he brought cupcakes and doughnut holes home for dessert. He kept the windows opened wide so the sun and plenty of air got in. And me and him played b-ball in the yard and finished sanding and refinishing them two cabinets my mother's been wanting done.

My mother stopped talking so much about Jason. And she wasn't cleaning his room as much as before. Maybe that's because she was getting ready for Kentucky. She wasn't gonna go once I got in trouble. But my father said she should. "That fight made Mann and me closer. With just us in the house, maybe we can get back to how we used to be."

"That's crazy, Mann." Kee-lee comes over every day now. "You eat somebody's finger and your parent's act like you got straight A's on your report card." He walks by my bed and picks up my paints. "You got these at Harold's? I been wanting to steal these." He sticks a brush in water and then in paint.

"Security's tight. Can't take nothing out that store."

He lies on the floor. Slides underneath a table I use for a desk and starts painting underneath it. We do that sometimes, when we don't want nobody to see the girls we drawing. "Your father acts like he's happy you messed Rock up."

I lie down by Kee-lee and draw a girl I saw a few days back. Only I make her hair down to her knees and give her a chest as big as plates, big purple lips, and a tongue that sticks out the side of her mouth like a sucker.

"Make her high yella. I like 'em like that," Kee-lee says.

I make her the color of my mom, brown like burned gravy. Kee-lee elbows me. I check out his girl. Her shorts look like Pampers. "Nice," I say, eyeing her thick legs, wondering how he makes 'em look so fine you wanna feel 'em up. I can't make legs like that. Mine come out like fat sticks. Kee-lee shows me what I'm doing wrong. Next thing I know my girl's got tight shorts on too and video-girl legs.

We got pieces of girls drawn under the desk: butts, lips, tits. Feet too. Kee-lee likes feet—long, skinny ones with polished toenails. I put an ankle bracelet on one foot, then blend orange and brown and make one of the butts wider. We don't talk for a while. We draw the kind of girls we see in magazines and wonder when we gonna get girls that look like them. Then we get out from under the desk and sit on opposite sides of the room and draw some more. My window's open. I see houses across the street and more houses up the hill. So I draw what I see, red bricks and burned chimneys; a man lying on a swing with a tan hat covering his face, and a woman reading the paper with her shoes off. I sketch leaning trees, speeding cars, broken screens hanging off doors, and a door being held open for a woman who's walking up the steps carrying groceries.

We ain't high; don't even try to smoke nothing. We don't eat; ain't even hungry after drawing two hours straight. We happy just showing each other how to get the right color gray sky or make steps that look like real people could walk right up 'em.

"Mann," Kee-lee says, holding his picture up to the light. "When we get our own studio, we gonna make a lotta dough." He holds my picture up next to his. "'Cause we good. We are so good."

He's right. We got skills, and one day the whole world's gonna know it.

Chapter 18

Y FATHER and me went fishing. He still wants me to stay close to home these days, so he didn't take me to the park to catch them. He brought the fish to me. He took a bucket and got hisself eight catfish out the pond in the park and dumped 'em in our tub. He tied a string to a stick. Put two stools in the bathroom and sat next to me for an hour and a half, talking and trying to get fish to eat stale corn curls dipped in bacon fat.

My mother's downstairs baking pies. Since I got out of juvey a month ago, she's been doing better. Every night she cooks supper and she and my dad clear the table together like they used to.

The psychologist's been asking me how things

are at home. It's hard to explain. Kee-lee's kind of right though. My dad is happy about what I did to Rock. My psychologist says that's disturbing. Yeah. No. I don't think he's glad I hurt Rock. I think he's glad that I won't let nobody try to get over on me.

"How does that make you feel?" she asked me the other day.

"Huh?"

"How does it make you feel knowing that your dad gets happy when you hurt people?"

Her office is for little kids, with jacks and checkers and playing cards the size of my hand. "It don't make me feel like nothing."

I lied when I said that, 'cause since I bit Rock, I sleep better. Kee-lee says it don't have nothing to do with Rock. "It's got to do with your dad. He ain't all wigged out now, so it makes things better for you."

I like my dad now. Sitting here fishing with him is the most fun thing we've done together since Jason died. There's pop in a cooler full of ice, and chips and tuna sandwiches sitting on plates on top of the toilet tank. "Don't let him get away!" My father's standing up, pulling back the stick; dangling the fish over the tub water. "Twenty bucks if you pick up a fish with your bare hands."

I'm broke. So I don't waste time reaching into the water with my hands and picking a fish up by the tail. "Forty bucks and I'll pick up five."

My dad's sticking his fish in the sink, pulling the hook out its mouth. "Make it six."

The tub is almost filled to the top. I get down on my knees and stick my arms in, spilling water all over the floor. I throw a fish at my dad. "Catch."

He laughs and ducks.

More fish are coming his way. "This one too." I'm pulling fish up by their tails and throwing them at him. They're hitting his chest and landing on the floor, sliding into the toilet. He's hopping around like a girl. Yelling for me to quit.

"Naw! I want my money!"

My shirt is soaked. My hands are slimy and the bathroom smells. I get up, then I slip and fall down next to a fish.

"What the . . . ?" My mother's at the door, shaking her head and laughing. Three more fish are flopping around the wet floor. My dad's holding one to his chest like a baby, saying I'd better watch out, 'cause he's gonna get me back for this. "You're not gonna know when or where." He laughs. "Maybe you gonna find a fish in your bed." He sets the fish in the tub water. "Maybe you gonna find a snake or a squirrel in your shorts." He grabs me by the shoulders and pulls me over to him. "You like squirrels, Mann? Pigeons walking on your head?" His arm goes around my neck and he gives my head a noogie.

I think about the psychologist. Tell myself to tell her how my dad used to play tricks on us; used to be our best friend.

He wipes his hands on my mom's apron, sits on the toilet, and pinches her butt. "How many fish you eating tonight, Grace?"

She's out the bathroom, standing in the hall. "Not a one. Better call Cousin and Ma Dear."

My father nods his head toward the door. I run and get the phone. Water rolls down my legs and soaks my sneakers. "Ma Dear," I say, when she answers. "We gonna have a fish fry."

Chapter 19

BOYS WILL DO anything if they think a girl is looking. That's how come I let Kee-lee talk me into doing this. If we hadn't done such a nice job, my mom woulda been sad and my father woulda been mad. But it was cool, what we did. And Keisha and her cousin who lives across the street liked us more because of it.

Kee-lee's been liking Keisha since they was eight. She used to be skinny, but since school ended, she got bigger—everywhere. That only made Kee-lee like her more. She can get any boy she likes now, "So why I want you?" she tells him sometimes. He don't mind her being mean, 'cause he figures she's gonna be his one day.

My mother was at the mall. Kee-lee and me was playing videos. Then we shot hoops. Then we sat outside on the curb talking to Keisha and Carlotta, who was supposed to be on punishment for sneaking out the house last night. Kee-lee started it. He asked Keisha, the pretty one, if she wanted to feel his hair. "It's good. Soft, too."

She told him no. Her cousin Carlotta told her she was chicken. Kee-lee bet Carlotta he could get Keisha to come across the street and play with his hair. She leaned over the railing, crossing her big pretty legs. "What you betting?"

Kee-lee started licking his lips and smelling his breath. "Let me see." He rubbed his muscles. "If I get Keisha to rub my hair, then you gotta kiss me." He stuck out his lips. "Right here. If I can't get her to come rub my curls, I'll carry you up the street and around the corner on my back."

Carlotta whispered in Keisha's ear. She looked at Kee-lee and said she'd take the bet. Keisha says she's not rubbing his head: he might have cooties in his hair. "So you might as well bend down and give Carlotta a ride."

It was on, then, 'cause Kee-lee don't let nobody talk about his hair.

I didn't see what Kee-lee could do to get the girl to rub his hair. And I didn't see why he wanted Carlotta to kiss him anyhow. She ain't cute. And she's not built as good as Keisha. But it turns out Kee-lee didn't care nothing about her anyhow. He was trying to make Keisha jealous. Hoping to get a kiss off her too.

It took Kee-lee a while to think of something to do to get that girl over to our side of the road. He ran in my house, came back with colored chalk, and started drawing right in the street. There was hardly any traffic on our block. So the picture he drew stayed fresh until he was done. It wasn't big enough for the girls to see the whole thing from across the street. But it was big enough for them to see that he was drawing their picture. Making them look exactly like they look in person, only he made Carlotta look better than she really does.

My mother pulled up to the house. She stopped and checked the picture out before it was done. She looked across the street at the girls. "Oh, you're gonna like this." She went inside with her bags.

The girls took their time crossing the street. But I could tell they wanted to rush. Kee-lee stopped them.

Said only Carlotta could come see. But she had to rub his head first. Kee-lee just changed the rules but Carlotta didn't care about rubbing his hair, long as she didn't have to kiss him. But Kee-lee said if she kissed him, he'd draw the same picture on paper for her. He'd frame it too. At first she said she didn't wanna kiss a boy with rotten teeth. But then she saw the drawing. Her hand covered her mouth. Her eyes bugged. "You did this? You?" she said, like she didn't just see him draw it.

Kee-lee didn't have to ask for no kiss. She closed her eyes and opened her mouth and, man—I sure wish that'd been me kissing her. Even though she ain't pretty, she's still a girl.

Keisha had her arms crossed at first. Then when the kissing didn't stop, she came over and pulled Carlotta off Kee-lee.

He winked. "I got bad teeth, but I got soft baby lips, now don't I?" He stepped up to Keisha. "Want some?"

She spit and told him to get out her face. But she didn't go nowhere. She stared at the street. "I want one on paper too, so I can have it forever."

Kee-lee was gonna draw one for her cousin, but if Keisha wanted one, he said, her lips were gonna have to pay up first. Keisha was looking at his teeth while he talked, frowning up her face. "Never mind," she said, folding her arms and turning away.

Carlotta whispered, but we still heard her. "Don't look at his teeth. Just kiss him." She turned around and rubbed Kee-lee's hair, and whispered too loud again. "He do got soft lips." Keisha licked her lips and stared at his mouth again. She didn't give him no warning. She pulled him over to her and stuck her lips out, closed her eyes, and made a face like she was swallowing bleach. She ain't stop kissing him for a while, then she wiped her lips and pushed him away. "Happy now?"

After Kee-lee gave them each a picture, they went back inside. It didn't take us long to get bored. That's when I got out my charcoals and crayons and started drawing. Kee-lee saw what I was doing and helped. When it was done, we had a big picture of Jason. It was just his face, and it wasn't gonna last once the rain came. But when my mother saw it, she got down on her knees and rubbed his cheeks and touched his big brown eyes. My dad said we did a good job. And when I went to bed later on that night, I saw him and my mom outside with the back light on, standing over Jason; holding each other, talking real soft and sweet. Waiting for the rain, I guess.

 WAS HOME ALL by myself. I saw what happened. A man with a gun walked up to a group of boys standing on our pavement talking, and pulled the trigger. *Bang!* When my mother and father get home, yellow tape ropes off our sidewalk so they have to walk around it. Blood from the boy who got shot is still on the ground.

"Let's go," my father says, pulling me up the steps by my arm.

When we get to my room, he pulls my dresser drawers open two at a time. Dumps clothes on the floor and then stuffs them in a large green plastic bag.

My mother walks in and grabs my father's hand. "What in the world?"

He pushes her hand away and walks out. Next thing I know he's in their bedroom, dumping plastic shavers, soap, and clothes in another green bag. "Get out my way, Grace," he says when she tries to block his way.

"William. You'd better tell me something."

He ignores her for a long while. Then when the bag's too heavy to drag or carry, he sits down on it. "They gonna kill him," he says, looking my way.

"Who? Why?"

I don't ask who. I figure somebody was coming for me sooner or later: a stranger, a friend— somebody.

My father starts talking about the murder right outside our front door. He says that's gonna be me one day. "He'll step on somebody's toe, or look at them too hard, or not do nothing to 'em, just be in the wrong place at the wrong time and, *Bang!*" he says, holding his throat and swallowing hard.

My mother makes me leave the room. But she don't shut the door all the way, so I hear her tell him what she told me not to tell him: she wants to move to Kentucky. She hadn't left yet because she was waiting for things to settle down with me. My dad says it won't do no good for me to go there unless I know how to defend myself. My mother says all we have to do is move someplace safe. "Then he'll be okay."

He sits her down on the bed next to him, touching her face and her lips. "Grace, don't you know that black boys is for hunting and killing and burying?" He gets quiet for a little while. Breathes deep and coughs. "And that don't change 'cause they got a new address."

He sticks his head out the door, points to the bag, and looks at me. "Take it downstairs."

The bag is way too heavy, but I don't say that. I pull. Drag. Sweat. Stop. Push. Kick that thing. I get it to the top of the steps. Stand in front. Hold on to the walls while it leans on the back of my legs. I take one step at a time and listen some more.

My father's talking again. Saying that a man is put on the planet to do two things—protect his family and make his boys into men. "Jason ain't never gonna be no man. But *he* is." He points my way, then pulls more bags into the hall. "But if he's gonna make it to manhood, he's gonna have to drop them daisies

I put in his hand." He cuts his eyes at me. "Forget what I said about treating people right and holding his tongue."

"William!"

My dad points directly at me. I step aside and let the bag roll down the steps. "If he's gonna grow into a man, he's gonna have to learn to chew nails and hold a gun in his hand, maybe even shoot somebody."

My mother's running down the stairs behind him. "William! You raised a good boy—good boys!"

My father ignores her. He heads for the living room and starts dumping bullets into a brown bag. My mother grabs the phone.

"Ma Dear," she says, dialing up my grandmother.

My father slams down the phone. "Ma Dear don't run my house!" He starts loading his gun. "How you gonna stop a man from protecting what's his?" He drops more bullets in the bag. "How a woman gonna teach a man how to raise a boy?"

My mother looks up when he says that. She stares at the phone, then goes to the kitchen. After my dad's done loading the truck, she comes back into the living room. She's got a box full of candy, chips, pretzels, and pop. "Here. Take these."

He hugs her, but before she lets him go, she asks him to promise her something.

"What?"

"That we will move to Kentucky if this thing you're doing with him doesn't work out."

My father always said it was hard for him to say no to my mother. I guess that's why he says yes. "But you gotta give me two weeks, Grace."

She looks at me and nods her head. "That's all you get, William. Two weeks. Then you'd better bring my boy back to me in one piece."

"In one piece," he says, walking over to her and holding her to him. "Maybe now's the time for you to go to Kentucky."

She's shaking her head no.

"I wouldn't hurt my own, Grace." He's whispering in her ear, saying he's just gonna teach me to box and hunt. "Toughen him up a little. That's all." He cuts on the porch light, then walks out the door, telling her to call my therapist and say that I'm sick.

One of Jason's soldiers is standing on the porch swing, with his rifle pointed at my father's back.

My mother hugs me and won't let me go, even while I'm trying to push her away.

"Go," she finally says, covering her mouth.

I don't move.

"Go," she whispers.

I swallow air.

Then Jason speaks up. Go.

I take a baby step.

Go, he says, giggling.

I take another step.

Go, dog. Go, he says.

I take off running across the floor with my eyes closed. Jumping. Flying high over the porch, landing on the concrete step on my own two feet. Like a man.

Chapter 21

Y FATHER IS not a talker. He can sit and be quiet for hours, so it's good that he talked Kee-lee's mom into letting him go too.

Kee-lee's in the backseat with the bags. "I'm tired."

I try to give my dad the hint. "Me too."

We been driving for four hours, nonstop. We're not in our city no more. We're on a highway passing trucks full of dirty chickens, stinking pigs as big as cows, and horses that shine like their coat's been greased with hair oil. "Mr. Adler," Kee-lee says. "I gotta pee. Now."

My father pulls the truck over to the side of the road. Kee-lee unzips his pants and hops out.

My dad points to a field full of grass. "Do your business over there."

Me and Kee-lee are looking at things flying and hopping around, and we don't move.

"Y'all go do your business. Now."

I'm not in that grass two minutes before three grasshoppers take a ride on my pants. Kee-lee hates bugs, so he's running around in circles like a girl. "Take it off, Mann! Take it off!" Slapping his legs, he drops his pants and trips over them. I'm laughing, holding a skinny light-green hopper in my hand. Walking up to Kee-lee with my mouth wide open. Bringing the hopper closer and closer to my stuck-out tongue.

"Aw, man," he says, turning away.

I smack my lips. "That was good," I say, chewing. I hold another hopper out to him. "Now you eat one."

He takes off running, falling down in the grass.

"You too scared to eat a bug?"

While he's peeing and yawning, I take that hopper and flick it in his mouth. Pee shoots everywhere. Kee-lee's slapping his tongue with his wet fingers.

Throwing half the hopper my way and spitting out legs and a head.

I'm slobbering over myself, I'm laughing so hard. Rolling around in the itchy grass and holding my side. Pointing to Kee-lee, who's laughing now too and can't stop.

"What?" my father asks, laughing hisself.

"Kee-lee ate . . ."

"What?"

"A hopper. A hopper was on my . . ."

We're all laughing, holding our sides and getting dust and grass stuck in our hair every time we move. After a while we lie on the ground with our hands under our heads, staring straight up at the sky. The clouds are white, like somebody stuck 'em in a washer and poured in extra bleach. The grass smells spicy, like them cardboard pine trees that hang in your car window. Already, I'm liking this trip.

It's August, so it stays light a long time. My father looks tired. He's been driving since yesterday. "How far we going?" I ask.

"Forever," he says.

Kee-lee yawns and stretches. He's covered in pink Calamine lotion to make the ant bites stop itching. He lay down in a patch of carpenter ants and they ate him up good.

My father picks up speed. "We need to find someplace to stay for the night."

I'm looking for a motel or hotel sign. Kee-lee's saying he ain't sleeping on no cot. He wants a real bed. My dad's not saying a thing. He's got country music on the radio and a cold beer between his legs. He points out the window. "There's a spot."

I don't see nothing, just grass and trees. I look across the road. There's a gray sign with sticks glued around it saying CAMPGROUND. SPACE FOR $20 A NIGHT.

Kee-lee tells my dad he ain't sleeping outdoors with bugs.

My dad pulls into the driveway and pays a fat white man at the gate. He drives into the campground with one hand, pointing to the back of the truck with the other. He lets us know he brought the grill, tent, cooler, and some food for us to eat. "We gonna do some good eating."

"Good eating?" Kee-lee and me both laugh.

"What's good eating?" Kee-lee asks.

"Anything you can catch: fish, possum." My father steps out the car.

Kee-lee takes one end of the cooler, I take the other. "Rats. I ain't eating no rats."

My dad's standing by the car with his arms folded and his sleeves rolled up. "Seems to me you'd take the tent out first." He looks up at the sky. "It gets dark fast in the woods. You wanna be setting up in pitch-black, worried about what's crawling over your fingers and into the tent?"

We drop the cooler, grab the tent, and help my father set up. I'm sticking poles in the ground and looking all around. The people next to us are white. The people across from us are white too. So are all the other people here. "They ain't gonna shoot us, are they?"

Chapter 22

T'S STILL GONNA be a while before it gets dark. So Kee-lee and me pocket a few rocks and set off walking. "To hit somebody," I say, "if they start something with us."

Neither one of us has ever been to a place like this. There's people everywhere: sitting outside of tents or in parked cars or vans, grilling stuff that smells so good it makes you wanna beg like a dog. Kids are everywhere too. Running. Laughing. Playing cards, catch and tag, hoola-hoop, b-ball, and jump rope, or just lying across somebody's lap, getting their hair braided. All the stuff we used to do round our way, till the killings started four years ago.

We head up a dusty trail that winds around the lake and lets you out near a field of trees so thick it shuts out almost all the light. We climb over rocks that look rusty from too much rain. I lie on my stomach. Look over the edge and drop stones into the muddy water. Kee-lee lights up a blunt. I lay my ear on the rock and listen. He shakes his head like I'm nuts. I take a hit. Hold the smoke in till I spit it out and cough my head off. Then I check out the water some more. It's just sitting there. Still. So gray you can't see to the bottom; so quiet it seems dead. I stand up and push Kee-lee in.

"Ma-a-ann!"

I dive in behind him. The water's warm, at first, like a nighttime bath in the wintertime. But the deeper I go, the cooler it gets. Stuff's floating and swimming past me. Sticks and string. Soft-shell turtles. Snakes. Go down some more, I tell myself. So I kick harder. Move my arms faster. Feel my baggy jeans get heavier when I go deeper.

Get yourself some air, I'm thinking. But the water's nice and cool now. I wanna bring myself something back from down here. So I pick up a slimy green rock and stick it in my pocket. Grab a little brown turtle and stick it down my drawers. Snatch a black baby snake that slides out my hand.

My lungs burn like hot wax got dripped on 'em, so I head up—fast. My mouth's trying to open. My nose is trying to suck in air. *You gonna die.* I'm telling my head to stop saying that. *You gonna drown.* My feet kick, but they don't get me nowhere. My arms are dropping as fast as books out a second-floor window. My eyes close and my nose is doing what it wants to—breathing.

"Mann!"

I'm coughing. Choking.

"Boy, open your eyes."

Kee-lee's laughing. Sitting on the short cliff, watching me cough up snot and spit.

"You wasn't down that far. I seen you the whole time." He kicks my sneakers in the water. "It's a lake. Not no ocean."

I grab my sneakers, walk over to the sand, and sit down. I unzip my pants and feel around in my shorts for the turtle. It's gone. I lie on my back and look up at the sky, watching a crop plane pulling a sign: BUY ONE GET ONE FREE, MASON'S GROCERY STORE.

Kee-lee's kicking sand. "Move over."

A spider crawls in between my fingers. A yellow jacket flies next to my ear, buzzing around my legs and feet. Me and Kee-lee just watch it. Then we both fall asleep, right there by the water—outside in public, not worrying about nobody bothering us.

Chapter 23

E SLEPT ON the ground last night. We were in sleeping bags. Had us some pillows too. But a pillow don't make the ground no bed. That's what I told my dad. He said for me to quit complaining. We been here two nights and I'm ready to go home. The bugs bite. The grill burns the eggs, and I'm tired of seeing trees and swimming in water that leaves your underwear brown.

My dad says not to complain, but he's still in the tent, sleeping. He tells us it's our turn to make breakfast, then he pulls the sleeping bag over his head. "Look around the place some more."

We saw everything already. Yesterday we swam in the lake. We walked until our feet hurt. Then we ran into a woman grilling corn on the cob, red potatoes, and shrimp. Kee-lee wasn't gonna pass that up, so he walked right up to her and introduced hisself. She and her sister liked him right off and set paper plates on their picnic table for us. We ate and drank till our stomachs hurt. Then we thanked them and left. Soon as we could, we found us a place to go to sleep. When we woke up four hours later, we were bored all over again. That's when Kee-lee came up with this idea—race up the tallest trees we could find.

I said okay. I mean, if he can do it, so can I. We shoulda went back to our tent, though. It was getting dark before we even started. And the trees are really tall here.

"First to the top gets five bucks," Kee-lee said.

I started up. Didn't wait for him to say go or nothing. Kee-lee don't like to lose. So he climbed the tree, two branches at a time. Walked up one branch that was thick as a bench and the next thing I knew I was looking up at him.

"That don't mean you gonna win," I said, sticking my foot in a hole the size of my head, ducking when bird poop dropped down on me. I pulled myself up by a branch and climbed up three more. The tree was tall as two houses stacked on top of each other. The branches were long as a car. Some were thick enough to climb; some were thin as wire. We're close to a forest, so there were lots of trees here blocking out the sky.

Kee-lee was sitting on a branch, kicking out his legs. "Give up yet?"

I started climbing again. "Never." I looked down at the ground. Couldn't hardly see it from the leaves in my way. I pushed back a branch. My stomach turned. "How far up you think we are?"

He leaned over, holding the trunk with one hand. "Far." He climbed some more. "But I like far." He stared up. "Too far ain't even far enough for me." He was yelling. I was yelling and watching the sky turn dark yellow, then fire orange. "It's gonna be dark soon. We better get down."

"Naw. I'm liking it here. Gonna climb till I touch the moon."

I looked down, but kept on climbing. I took my left leg, stretched it out, and held on tight to the branch over head.

"Mann! I'm falling. I'm—"

Kee-lee ain't never gonna be no actor. "Shut up." I leaned over. He was up, way up. High as a rooftop. "All right. You win. I ain't going that high."

He started down, climbing like a spider on the run. Jumping from branch to branch. I was taking my time. Careful not to fall.

A half hour later, I'm still in the tree, trying to get down. Kee-lee was on his second blunt. "I'll get your father," he said, lying back in the grass and staring at the sky. "Hey. I didn't know stars come out before dark."

I told him not to get my dad, because he'd be mad when he saw I was too scared to get myself out that tree.

Kee-lee was tracing stars with his fingers. "How they got more stars out here than we got back home?"

I smashed a red beetle with my thumb. I looked up. It was like every star in the galaxy was right here. I checked out the ground again. If I jumped, I was gonna break something. If I didn't jump, my father was gonna break something on me.

"Jump," Kee-lee said. "I wanna see what happens." He was laughing. Throwing a stick at a brown spotted frog. Saying he was gonna make me eat it when I got down.

"Ready," I said, watching campfires light up like candles on a cake. "Set," I said, praying to Jason to make my bones stay put when they hit the ground, "Go! . . ."

"Boy! You out your mind?" It was my father. He was carrying the brown bag. The one with the gun and knives in it. He's gonna shoot me down, I thought.

"Get down. Now!"

I told him I couldn't come down. I didn't say I was scared. But he knew.

People didn't notice me all that much before my dad came along. Now they were stopping and staring. Offering to help. "No. No. We just fine," he said to them. Then he told me to come down. I tried. But my foot slipped and I fell down three branches and cut my cheek.

"I'll get him," a boy said, starting up the tree.

My father held the boy's shoulder tight. "Naw. He can do it."

Women with long, stringy hair and sad faces shook their heads and whispered. Kee-lee was lying on the ground, watching me one minute and pointing up to the sky the next. "Hey, Mann. Ain't that the Big Dipper?"

People got tired of watching and waiting, so there wasn't nobody around after a while. Just me, my dad, Kee-lee, and the boy who'd said he'd climb to get me. "Well, you gonna get cold but you won't die." My father patted Kee-lee on the shoulder and told him to come on. "Food's cold now. And I'm sleepy."

"Don't go!"

"Men don't . . ."

"I ain't no man!"

My father put the brown bag under his arm and kept walking. "Kee-lee. Do like I say, boy."

Kee-lee hunched his shoulders and followed my dad. The boy skipped after them. Before long, the sky was dark except for the stars and the moon. Things crawled over my fingers and walked on my head. They whistled, and they clicked like the hands on a stopwatch, and they scratched like a mouse in a drawer. I reached for another branch. Stretched my leg out and stepped down onto a limb that cracked like an old egg. I was falling, feeling sticks dig into my ankles and arms and rip holes in my shirt and shorts.

But I didn't hit the ground. I held tight to another branch. I stepped down, stepped over, stepped on branches. I heard owls. I heard things sliding across water, hopping in the grass, and listening like they was gonna tell what they heard later on. I leaned on the tree trunk. Held it tight. Reached my foot way down. Grabbed a branch. Stepped over two more. Wiped a six-legged black bug off my arm. Kicked at a squirrel that wouldn't get out my way. I held on to the tree trunk. Slid down. Scratched my face. Jumped to the ground.

It was pitch-black out, but up the road just a little, I saw campfires, and lanterns hanging from campers. I brushed wood off my clothes and out my hair. Wiped blood off my face and felt around for bumps and bites I got all over me. Then I headed for the light, walking slow; dipping low like the men round my way always do.

Chapter 24

"SHOOT!"

I close my eyes, point the gun, and almost squeeze the trigger. "I—I—can't."

Kee-lee runs up to me. "Let me shoot. I ain't scared."

We are outside the campgrounds, in the woods. My father is sitting on a stump, shaking his head at me. He makes me step aside so Kee-lee can take his turn.

Kee-lee licks his lips. "All ri-i-ight." He closes one eye. "I always wanted to pop a cap in somebody." He holds both arms straight and tight, and points the gun at the target my father made—a head made of stuffed newspaper, with blueberry eyes and sticks for hair.

Bang!

My ears ring. *Bang!* My eyes close. *Bang, bang, bang!* I'm watching Jason in that little white casket, in that little white suit—smiling. "I'll be back," I say, running into the woods.

Kee-lee's right behind me. "You shoulda done it. It was sweet."

I bend down and pick up a daddy longlegs. "I don't like guns." He crawls up my finger.

"You ain't gotta like a gun to shoot one."

Bang, bang, bang, bang, bang.

Kee-lee runs. "Let's see if your dad killed something." He stops when he sees I ain't moving. "He mighta got a raccoon." He's up the road and back before I take a step. "He just blew the face off the paper head is all."

I sit it in the grass and set the daddy longlegs free. "Moo Moo . . ."

Kee-lee sticks sunflower seeds in his mouth. "Moo Moo's dead." He takes his arm and holds it out. Closes his eyes and shoots. "If he had a gun, he would still be living."

"Jason . . ."

"Why you all the time gotta talk about dead people?" He spits the shells out. Then he tells me that I'm lucky to have a father trying to teach me how to protect myself.

I walk behind a gray rabbit hopping into the bushes. Kee-lee follows me, only not too close. He says he's sorry Moo Moo's gone. "But I ain't dead. Don't wanna die neither."

The rabbit looks back at me, shakes like it's wet, and runs. Kee-lee says he don't wanna hurt me, but he's gonna if I don't stop playing with critters. He pushes back some bushes. Bends down low. Grabs a rock. "Let's knock it out and then shoot it."

It's a baby rabbit, so I catch it quick, and tell Kee-lee to carry it back. He's scared, like I figured. So I turn the rabbit loose. "You too scared to carry it, but you wanna kill it. That ain't right."

The rabbit runs under a bush. Me and Kee-lee go back to my dad. My palms are sweaty. The tip of my nose is wet. My throat is so dry, words won't come out. So I just hold out my hand, and tell it to quit shaking, when my father puts the loaded gun in it.

"Morning," the man in the camper across from us says. He's old. White and old and full of questions my father ain't up to answering. So that means me and Kee-lee gotta talk to him and his wife.

He's sitting in a green lawn chair with his pink, wrinkled legs spread open. "Been camping before?"

I dump coals on the grill. "No."

"No? Well, you haven't lived then."

He and his wife got on matching shorts. Blue veins run up and down her legs like lines on the map we used to get here. "We already ate. Pancakes, sausage, eggs . . ."

Her husband walks over and starts lighting our grill, even though I ain't ask him to. "Hot black coffee first thing in the morning while you're camping. Now, you can't beat that."

My father is reading the sports section, acting like them people ain't here.

"They got any stores around here?" Kee-lee asks. "I want some orange soda and a glazed doughnut." He digs in his pocket and pulls out one little sunflower seed. "Mr. Adler, I need some seeds."

"Oh," the old lady says, holding on to the chair and trying to stand up. "I have some. Lots."

Her feet hardly leave the ground when she walks, so dirt follows her wherever she goes. "Told you I had plenty," she says coming back outside and handing Kee-lee a fat brown bag.

He's smiling. Digging his fingers in the bag. "Thanks," he says, throwing seeds in his mouth. "Ill! What's these?" He drops the bag and seeds fly. "Bird seed? I don't want no bird seeds."

The old man's name is Ralph. He laughs. Walks over to my father and asks if he can sit down. The old lady's name is Sara. She tells Kee-lee they ain't for eating. "They're for the birds."

Sara sits back down. I take out one of my mother's frying pans and set it on the grill. Kee-lee spoons lard in the pan, since we forgot butter. I crack open five eggs, stir them up with salt and pepper, and pour them in the pan. Next thing I know, black smoke is covering the pan and choking my dad and Ralph. The pan is too hot, so in a few minutes, our eggs look like bubbly black tar.

Ralph thinks everything's funny. "Won't be the last time you burn your food out here. Camping takes some getting used to."

My father shakes his head. "No breakfast, I guess."

"We have lots of eggs," Ralph says.

My dad talks real low so Ralph don't hear. "A black boy don't get a hundred chances to get it right.

Sometimes he just gets one. That's it." The veins on the side of his head push out. "You blow your chance, you blow your life."

Kee-lee opens the truck door and looks inside. "I'm hungry. Where's the peanut butter?"

Them old people won't stay out of our business. Sara lets us know she's got leftover sausage and plenty of cinnamon toast and warm honey.

I look at my dad. "No, thanks," I say, even though cinnamon toast is my favorite.

Kee-lee walks over to her. "I want some."

He's gonna catch it, I'm thinking. But Sara's kicking up dust again. Holding out her hand so Kee-lee can help her. Ralph is right behind them. "Come on in," he says, waving me and my dad over. "We've got plenty of room inside."

My father tells him no. He wants me and him to go fishing instead. Kee-lee's in the camper. I'm headed for the truck, pulling out our rusted fishing rods. Listening to Ralph try to talk my dad into letting me eat breakfast before we go. My father don't answer him. He goes in the tent to change and heads for the lake. For a little while, I just watch him go. Then he yells for me to come on—now. I follow. But all the while I'm thinking, If you drown in that lake, it would be all right with me.

HERE'S MEN IN boats way out in the middle of the lake. And there's little boys standing in the water between their fathers' legs, holding fishing rods twice their size. Me and my dad fished like that once when I was little. He dressed me while I was still asleep, drove me to a lake outside of town, and him and me fished till the sun came up.

"Catch something," my dad tells me. He walks into the water till it's up to his thighs. He's got on boots and plastic pants. He tells me to come. I don't want to. I'm wearing Timberlands and I don't want my feet getting wet. He walks deeper into the lake. "You scared of guns. Don't like water. What are you, a girl?"

I step into the cold water, thinking about the fishing we did in the bathtub. Thinking about the fishing we did when I was little. Wondering why my father got me out here now, when he knows ain't no fish jumping this time of day.

Sand slides into my boots and floats between my toes. Mosquitoes stick to my neck and crawl up my arm. After a while, I'm picking gnats out my ear like wax. "The water's too cold."

My dad pulls me by the arm. "Get over here!"

I shove him. He shoves me back. Hard. I fall into the water. I stay down longer than I gotta because I don't wanna come up and be with him. But when I do, my dad's got the fishing pole high up in the air like a switch. "Boy, don't make me . . ."

Before Jason died, my father never hit me. He carried me on his shoulders and bought me paints from the old garage where his friend worked sometimes. He never hollered. He was as quiet as one of Jason's plastic soldiers.

I walk into the water up to my waist. Things slide in between my legs and bite me under my ribs. Red bumps pop up like measles, but I don't say nothing.

I keep the pole in the water three hours straight, not talking to my dad, not complaining, not having fun neither.

I'm shaking when I get out. Pulling green slime off my skin and scared to look too long at the red welts on my arms.

"I seen you in the water," Kee-lee says. "So I took off the other way." He's got red candy stuck to the front of his teeth. "Candy apple," he says, picking it off. "Sara makes them." He pats his stomach. "That white lady can cook!" He digs in his pocket. "She made me pancakes and sausage. Gave me lunch too."

I ain't ignoring Kee-lee, I'm just watching my father. He's walking in front of us, carrying both the poles. No fish though. Three hours and no fish. When we get back to camp, Ralph says he coulda told my father wasn't nothing biting this time of day. "Gotta get there well before the sun shows itself," he says, inviting us to a fish supper with them.

"We got plenty of food."

Sara pushes my dad out the way. "Oh, Lord. Ralph, get some iodine." She's touching my legs. Pulling my shirt up.

"It hurt?" Kee-lee asks.

"Ralph!" Sara yells. "Go next door and borrow more iodine. Cotton balls too." She grabs my hand and pulls me. "He's warm, you know." She stares back at my father. "Got a fever from the heat or the bugs."

My father is taking off his boots. Sitting down and looking tired. "He'll be all right."

"He's *not* all right! He's hurt. And you should be ashamed of yourself."

My father's eyes roll. "Lady . . ."

"Sara!" she says, opening the door. "My name is Sara."

"Well, *Sara*," he says, pulling off a boot and throwing it in the dirt. "Boys round our way don't die from bug bites. They die because . . ."

Sara keeps her back to him. "Boys are not supposed to die." She takes my hand. "They're supposed to grow into fine young men."

My father throws his other boot and knocks over the grill. Coals and ashes fly. "Get over here. Now."

Ralph speaks up. "Now, William . . ."

My father's toes and feet turn gray when he walks through the ash and up Sara's steps. He pulls me by the arm. "He's fine."

Sara won't turn me loose. "He's sick. And you—"

"Lady . . . Don't."

Ralph's standing up now, and people walking by are staring. Wondering, I bet, what this black man's doing yelling at a little old white lady. If we was home, the police would be here and my father would be in 'cuffs. "It's all right, Sara. The itching's stopped anyhow." I twist my hand free from hers and walk toward my father.

"It's gonna rain tonight," she says. "He ought to be inside. Dry. Not in *that* tent."

My dad keeps walking. Me and Kee-lee know better than to say one word to him, so we shut our mouths and follow him to our side of the road. Sara's right though. Our tent ain't made of much. It's old and taped in spots.

"It ain't gonna rain too hard," Kee-lee says, looking up to the sky. "Is it?"

I keep walking, acting like I don't see black clouds moving round overhead.

Chapter 26

OOM! BOOM!

I close my eyes and try to act cool, but who wants to be in a tent when it's storming. This isn't even our tent. It's an old army tent borrowed from a neighbor who hasn't used it in ten years, so there aren't any vents to look out and see what's really going on.

Boom!

My fever is worse. I know that even without a thermometer. I'm hot, wet, and sweaty—shivering too.

Boom! The ground shakes when thunder and lightning hits.

"You okay, boy?" my father asks. He's lying next to me right on the wet cold ground. Earlier, he put his sleeping bag over me. "To take away the chill."

"I'm fine." I turn to Kee-lee. "You okay?"

"When we going home?" he asks.

Boom!

We both jump. I close my eyes and listen to our jar fill up with water pouring from a hole in the top of the tent.

Pow! Snap!

Something got hit. A tree, most likely. My dad unzips the tent and sticks his head out.

I crawl over to him and stare out too. It's raining sideways. Branches as tall as my dad are lying across the road, or hanging from trees like broken arms.

"Where they going?" I ask. A man is running with his wife and kids to the car. Other people run by us, slipping and falling in the mud. Dripping wet. Looking scared.

Kee-lee elbows me in the back. "They getting outta here."

My dad tells us not to worry. They are just waiting the storm out in their cars. He puts on his shoes and sticks his wallet in his back pocket. He throws socks at me and a green plastic jacket Kee-lee's way. "I'll pull the truck in front of the tent and blow the horn for you two." We're not leaving, he tells us. We'll just dry out in the truck.

The truck is a few trees over. My dad says to give him a few minutes to warm it up and clear the leaves off. I change outta my wet socks and pants.

Boom!

"Don't be gone long," Kee-lee says, even though my dad's already gone. He's shaking, but I can't tell if it's from the cold rain or because he's scared. He pulls his pants on over his pajamas and frowns when he puts his soggy sneakers on. "If your dad don't know nothing about camping, why he bring us out here?"

I'm listening for the horn. But all I hear is thunder and lightning, people yelling at each other, and every once in a while, girls screaming.

"We're by the forest, you know. Trees everywhere." Kee-lee sticks a flashlight down his pants. It's shining up in his face. "Lightning's got a thing for trees. And trees don't mind falling on people and killing them."

I wish he would shut up.

After a long while, he unzips the tent. "Maybe the truck won't start." Rain blows inside.

"Close it!"

He steps outside. Me too.

"I don't see the truck."

Rain hits me like sticks. I open my mouth and it blows in. I look up and down the road, and it pours in my eyes so I can't see. Kee-lee looks down at me. "He left us!"

"No . . ."

He points to tire tracks.

I see 'em leading up the road. "He'll be back."

Cars start up and headlights go on. People run, holding on to their kids. Me and Kee-lee stand stuck in the rain like totem poles and try to figure out what to do.

Chapter 27

E LEFT US. He took the truck and left us in the pouring rain and mud with nothing to eat, no money, and no way home. Me and Kee-lee know it's true because the truck was parked not far from the tent. Now it's gone.

My father's been gone all night. Long enough for the rain to stop, my fever to end, and for people to come out their cars and tents and start picking up what the rain knocked down.

"It's a mess. But the sky's always prettier after a good hard rain," Sara says, looking up. She's walking in the mud in her green granny boots, filling trash bags with leaves and dead animals that the rain washed in front of their camper. "Where's your father?"

Kee-lee looks at me. He lies. He says he's up the road using his truck to pull somebody's car out a ditch. I'm picking up rocks and dead frogs, birds with busted wings, and bugs I ain't never seen before, and throwing them into a patch of trees behind our tent.

Sara looks up and down the road. "You've got quite a mess to clean up here." She presses her hand to my forehead. "Your fever's gone, so you'd best go looking for your dad."

Kee-lee looks at me. "Yeah. We better."

Sara puts ham and sausage on the grill. "Your father won't have time to cook up a decent meal." She reminds me of Ma Dear when she takes my hand. "We have room if you want to take a nap right after you eat."

I follow Kee-lee up the road. Him and me spend a long time looking for my dad. It's hard walking with mud sticking to your sneakers, and leaves and trees blocking every step you take. People are wringing water out of clothes and hanging them up on lines, across trees, and on top of running cars. Kids are sliding down mud hills and making mud pies and having mud fights. "He took off and left us," Kee-lee says again.

I'm standing in the middle of the road, trying to figure out what to do. We tell Sara or anyone else my father took off and they gonna call the state on us. We ask to use their phone to call my mom or Ma Dear and the state's gonna show up before anyone else can come get to us. "We gotta act like we found him," I tell Kee-lee. "Act like we found him and he was going to drive somebody off the campground to get something."

Kee-lee's making mud balls and throwing 'em at kids he don't know. "Tomorrow, when he's still gone, they gonna know he left us."

He's right. So we gotta be gone in the morning, before everybody else wakes up, I tell him. He wipes his runny nose with the back of his hand. Mud smears across his face. "We don't know where we at though."

"So?"

"And we don't have no money."

"So?"

"And . . ."

"Shut up, Kee-lee."

When we get back to Sara's place, we tell them the story we made up. She lets us eat in her camper. Man, she can cook. Cheese grits, sausages, scrambled eggs, pancakes, syrup, apple juice, and sticky buns. When we done, all we can do is sleep, right there on the floor. We play Tonk when we wake up. Come supper time, my dad's still gone. Me and Kee-lee look for him again and come back with another lie. Sara and Ralph look at each other, but they don't say nothing.

"Glad for the company," Ralph says, pulling back a kitchen chair so Sara can sit down.

Kee-lee's doing just like me, licking his lips and forgetting his manners. Reaching halfway across the table and picking up the hot fried chicken with his fingers. Dropping three pieces on his plate.

"Can I have two biscuits?" I ask. "And . . ."

Sara smiles. She reaches for my plate. When she's done, I got mashed potatoes, fried fish, and okra piled on my plate. Sweet tea sits in a plastic pitcher in the middle of the table. It's gone ten minutes later.

After we eat, we try to find my dad again. The sun's going down. Campfires are burning and families are all together. Kids laugh, holding marshmallow sticks over red-hot fires. Me and Kee-lee keep walking, even though we know my dad ain't never coming back.

Chapter 28

RALPH FORCED US into letting him help us find my dad. He said something wasn't right, and he was gonna get to the bottom of things. It was eleven at night. He said it wasn't right for him to be gone all day long, not even to help out other folks. So he made us get in the truck with him. For the last hour we've been circling the campground. "I hate to say this," Ralph says, scratching his bald head, "but do you think he took off?"

We both say it together. "No."

Kee-lee sticks half his body out the window and

yells, "He's here. But it's dark. We can't tell where we saw him last."

Ralph drives real slow, rolling over sticks and dead things and through mud so deep the car spins it all over the place. He turns the car around. "I guess he could still be out here, but he ought to be with you two."

When we get to the camper, Sara says for us to sleep over. But we go back to our tent. It smells like an old basement. "I'm sleeping in my clothes," Kee-lee says.

"Me too."

We put down the clean, dry blankets Sara gave us and lie on top of them. We keep the flashlights on, making shadow puppets on the ceiling. We're leaving this place by sunup.

Kee-lee says he's ready to go home anyhow. I ask him how far he thinks we are from home. He don't answer. When I ask again, I hear snoring. I come out from under the covers and start packing stuff. We can't take everything. So I roll up my father's sleeping blanket. Put two water jugs in my backpack. Dump Kee-lee's stuff on the floor and pack up as much candy and food as I can, which ain't much. I lie down. Cover up and turn over. "What the—" It's one of Jason's toy soldiers, lying on the ground.

* * *

"Let's go."

The sun is almost up. Campfires are nothing but smoke. "I said, let's go."

Kee-lee wipes his baggy eyes and feels around inside his pajamas. "I gotta go," he says, opening the tent flap and whizzing. He wipes his fingers on his pajamas and lies back down.

"I told you—shhh! Quiet." I'm walking over to the tent door and looking out. It's Ralph. He's outside watching the sun come up, I guess. "See? You took too long."

Kee-lee wants to go back to sleep. I kick him. He turns over. He don't care if they call the police. He figures the cops will just call our moms. "The police never call your parents first. They call the state. They put you someplace where your parents can't find you. They ask you stuff you can't answer. . . ."

He sits up. "How do you know?"

"I just know."

Ralph's gone, so Kee-lee puts on his clothes and picks up his backpack and a roll of toilet tissue.

"I said, let's go!"

"I ain't using leaves like they do in the movies." He steps out back and does his business. He comes back in and grabs the brown paper bag.

I make him drop it. "No guns."

"We might need it," he says, sitting the bag on the ground.

I kick it to the side of the tent and tiptoe outside. I run up the hill, fast as I can. Kee-lee takes a while, but then he's right beside me, shooting his mouth off, like usual.

Chapter 29

BET IT'S A hundred degrees today. The sun is white as milk, and you can't look into it without your eyes watering. There's a ripped-up T-shirt covering Kee-lee's big head. And he's got his thumb sticking out, trying to hitch a ride. I keep walking, squeezing water out of a plastic bottle over my head and down my throat.

By lunchtime, all our water's gone. So are half a box of marshmallow crunch cereal and four apples. The sleeping bags are half a mile back. They got too heavy. Anyhow, we figure it won't be a long time before somebody picks us up and we get home.

Ain't nothing out here to take your mind off things; just trees and a dusty road—South White Rock Road—that don't nobody hardly drive up. I look back at the extra clothes I left in the middle of the road. "My father might still come for us."

Kee-lee gets mad. "Your dad's gone. He left us, same as mine."

I remind Kee-lee that his dad got shot. He reminds me that he took off long before the bullet found him.

Something musta happened to my dad. He wouldn't just take off, I think.

Kee-lee sits his backpack down in the middle of the road. "He planned it all along."

I drop my things too.

"Figured he ain't want no children at all. So he left you—and your mother too."

The road is hot. You can feel the heat up through your sneakers. "Take it back." I'm talking to Kee-lee and looking around at signs. SOUTH JENSON COUNTY ROUTE 46 N. HOTELS 20 MILES.

He swings at me and misses. "He dumped ya. That's what they all do."

144

My first punch lands right where I want—upside Kee-lee's big block head. His hands go up. I double punch him in the stomach, hoping his guts bust open and spill out all over the road like chitlins. When I'm done with the next punch, Kee-lee's got a bloody nose and a headache too I bet. But he ain't no quitter. So he wipes blood away with the rag on his head, holds his arms out straight as a row of corn and knocks his fists into the sides of my head. I fall to my knees.

"What you gotta say now?"

I'm down awhile. Opening and closing my eyes, trying to see straight. Grabbing him by the knees, bringing him down too. Rolling around, punching him. Ducking when he swings. Trying not to holler when he shoves my chin back so hard it feels like my head's gonna pop off.

"Ouch!"

He flips me over. Sits on my back and holds my face down. The tar feels like scalding-hot coffee. My head comes up. He pushes it back down. "I'm gonna kill you!" Kee-lee flips me, then he stands with his big foot on my stomach and smiles right before he stomps me.

Beep. Beep. Beeep.

A truck's coming. I don't see it because it's behind me. But I know it's a truck because my uncle drives one and he lets me pull the horn when I want.

"You gonna get run over," Kee-lee says, holding me down with his foot.

I twist his leg and try to take him down. His foot presses down on me. I'm kicking the air and punching the ground, listening to the truck roll closer. "Let me up!"

He wants me to say I'm sorry. To say my father left me like his father left him. But boys round my way never say they sorry.

Beeep! Beeep!

I look over my shoulder. The truck is so close I can see the driver. He can see us too. But he ain't slowing down.

Beeep!

Kee-lee screams. "Say it!"

The truck's an eighteen-wheeler. It's red with a slamming silver grill and smoking pipes.

Beeep!

"Say it!"

Stones on the ground jump like popcorn in a popper.

I look at Kee-lee looking at the truck.

"Just say it. Say . . ." He jumps off me and takes off running.

"Kee-lee!"

"Run, Mann! Run!"

The side of the road seems like it's ten blocks away. But we both get to it at the same time, jumping over the guardrail and into weeds tall as Jason.

Beep! Beep! Beeeep! The driver gives us the finger when he flies by

We give it right back to him.

Chapter 30

"E WAS GONNA kill us," Kee-lee says. "Run us over."

I wipe my sweaty forehead with the back of my arm. "And I thought people in the country were supposed to be nice." I climb over the guardrail behind Kee-lee and back on to the road.

We're trying to figure out where we're at. The road is long and winding. There's signs pointing the way to gas stations and restaurants, but we don't see no houses or buildings nearby, just trees and grass.

Kee-lee rips his T-shirt again and hands me a

piece. We tie our heads up. "Maybe we should get off the road," he says. "Walk in the woods for a while."

But we don't do nothing different. We keep walking along the road. We throw rocks and figure we'll be home by the time it's dark. When it's time to rest, we sit by a creek filled with pebbles and just enough water to cover our hot feet. It runs along the side of the road. Dry weeds and hundreds of purple flowers make it so you can't hardly see it. We wet ourselves down, fill our water bottles, and sit for a while.

We on our way again, sweating like usual, throwing stones at each other. Eating warm jelly sandwiches and licking the last of the melted chocolate M&M's from the bags. Then a blond-haired girl in a red convertible stops and asks if we're okay. She's driving a Mercedes-Benz sports coupe, wearing diamond earrings and a thick gold necklace.

"We all right," I say, still walking.

"No we ain't."

The girl's name is Amy. She's a college student at Brown and her dad runs the bank in town. "I don't live that far from here. You can get a bite to eat and call your folks."

Kee-lee's in the car already, messing up her white rugs with his dirty sneakers.

"No thanks, ma'am," I say again. "But you got a cell phone we can use?"

She pulls to the side of the road and hands me a phone. Kee-lee asks if she got a spare bedroom where we can sleep tonight. My father answers the phone. He says that Kee-lee and me ain't that far from home. That we can make it back on foot in a couple of weeks. I hold out the phone and stare at it like it's his face I'm seeing. "What?" I put it to my ear. "Y'all come and get us!"

"Boy," he says, "you're all right. Kee-lee too." He ain't asking me if I'm okay, he's telling me.

"It's steaming hot and we're hungry. And it's gonna be dark soon."

I tell my father to put my mother on the phone. He won't. Can't. "She's gone, remember? To Kentucky." He had it planned all along. He was gonna take us to the campground and leave us. Then we'd have to find our way back. "Like African boys do."

"Like Africans? We ain't no Africans!"

"Who African?" Kee-lee's drinking Perrier water and rubbing suntan lotion on his arms.

My father says he got the idea from a television

show he saw on African boys. That's when he asked Cousin to bring him books on the subject. "In some African villages, they leave boys alone in the forest for months so they will learn to be men."

"Months?"

"Months. Years. Whatever it takes."

"You ain't coming to get us? Never?"

"Never?" Kee-lee says, jumping outta the car and snatching the phone from me. "My mother's gonna kill you."

Kee-lee puts my dad on speaker phone. My father says that his mother knows all about it. That him and her agreed that if we stayed in the neighborhood, we'd get shot dead.

"But we gonna get killed out here too," Kee-lee says, pointing up the road. "A truck almost done us in. Lightning almost hit me in the head," he lies.

Amy keeps asking what the problem is and how come our parents won't come and get us. I don't answer because I'm listening to my dad. "I put a cell phone in the brown bag. You can use that when you need to get in touch."

"We ain't got the brown bag. I left it," I say, walking a few steps, then back, then up again. I whisper. "There was a gun in that bag."

My dad tells me that his grandfather was sixteen when he took an eighteen-hour train ride from Georgia up north all by hisself. I tell him that this ain't the olden days.

"He didn't have enough money for the trip at first, so he had to earn it. Pick cotton. Slop hogs. Husk corn."

"Come and get me!"

"Yeah," Kee-lee says into the phone.

My dad says if I do this, I'll never be scared again. I'm quiet. Thinking. "You scared . . . all the time now.

"You walk a hard enough road, and it'll make you a bitter man—I mean, a better man," my dad says.

"Huh?"

"Nothing. Just something I read once."

I'm sitting down. Watching Kee-lee slide into the front seat next to Amy. Listening to the radio go from country, to opera, to rap. "How far are we from home?"

"Two weeks by foot," my father says. "You can do this."

"Little boy," Amy says, "I have to go."

"We ain't got no way to contact you," I say. "We ain't got the bag."

Kee-lee pulls out the bag. He takes out the gun. "Nice, huh?" he says to the girl.

She starts the car up. "Get out! Now! And give me my phone!"

Kee-lee's laughing. Thinking it's funny. Pointing it her way. "We ain't gonna hurt you, girl."

Amy's screaming. My father's asking me what's going on. "Nothing. We gotta go. We'll call later."

I throw the phone at her.

She's fingering the numbers. "I'm calling the police."

Kee-lee grabs the brown bag, then reaches down and knocks the phone out Amy's hand. I grab the backpack and take off running. "Don't call the police! Please don't call!" I say, running into the middle of the road, almost getting run over by a truck full of cows.

Chapter 31

"**W**HAT'S THAT!?**" Kee-lee's almost sitting in my lap. "And that?" He's holding tight to the brown bag. "I can't see nothing. Light a match! Start a fire!"

I'm feeling round inside my backpack, blinking my eyes. Striking a match. Watching it go right out.

Hoo . . . hoo . . . hoo . . . Owls have big eyes. Big mouths too. Hoo . . . hoo . . . hoo . . .

Bang!

The gun is so close to my ear I can't hear nothing for a few minutes. "Kee-lee!"

Bang!

Kee-lee's shot the owl. He's shot something that ran past our feet too. I think it was a possum. Its insides have busted and spilled out like sloppy joes made with too much sauce. Smoke from the gun floats like steam. My whole body's shaking, like it did that time I had a fever and my mother made me sit in a tub of ice.

"Call my mother," Kee-lee says. "Call my mother now!" He's got the gun pointing at me. His finger's on the trigger.

I hand him the cell. He don't take it. He says for me to dial his mom. He's almost in tears when I put the phone up to his ear. "It's dark. And we ain't got a bed, or tent, or nothing."

I turn the flashlight on. Walk over to a tree bent down low. I break off branches and pull off flowers and make a tiny teepee with them. Kee-lee's mother's saying what my father said, I guess; because he's trying to get her to understand that this ain't right. That they don't know what it's like being out here alone. I pile leaves in the middle of the teepee and light a match.

Kee-lee's screaming at his mom. "How we gonna call you? The cell phone's almost dead."

He's threatening her. Holding the gun in the air and waving it. "I'm going to the police then," he says, walking back and forth. "Telling them how y'all treating us."

His mom hangs up on him. I call Cousin. His line is busy. I call my dad again. I ask him to come get us in the morning. I forget the name of the road we're on, but we can get someone to tell us. At first I think he's coming, because he asks if I left a trail on the way in. If I saw any guideposts. Then he says what he said before, what Kee-lee's mother said: "You gonna be all right."

Kee-lee and me keep seeing things: short fat things running deeper into the woods like they being chased. Big things—wolves, deer, a baby bear even, at least that's what we think. "Something's gonna eat us out here."

My father laughs. "Where you from, boy?"

Before I can answer he's asking another question. "Where are you at?"

I look around. "I don't know."

"Yeah you do."

I try to give him the answer he wants. Before I do, he's asking more questions.

"Would I do anything to hurt you?"

I ain't sure.

Kee-lee sits by the fire, pointing the gun at a deer stopped across the road.

"Don't . . ."

Bang!

When Jason got shot, his eyes got big, just like that deer's.

"What the . . ."

My father wants to know what happened. I tell him that Kee-lee shot at a deer and missed. He says for me to put Kee-lee on the phone. When he's done, Kee-lee puts the gun in the bag, the bag inside two T-shirts, and the T-shirts in the bottom of his backpack.

"You're on an adventure, boy," my father tells me.

I whisper so Kee-lee don't hear. "I'm lost. Scared."

"When you were here, you were lost . . . a boy who was gonna die a boy."

"I do all this," I shout, "and get back home and still they might just kill me." I remind my dad that stuff like that happens all the time. Somebody joins the army. They get out, come home, and get shot for sneakers or a jacket or a dime the crook found in the corner of their pocket.

"Yeah," he says. "Stuff like that can happen. But—"

I push the power button. I take the phone and throw it as far as I can.

Kee-lee takes off after it. "Why you do that? Now we can't get nobody to come get us." He don't go far. He's too scared.

I throw more sticks in the fire. "It don't matter. Nobody's coming for us nohow."

Chapter 32

OBODY'S GONNA pick up two black boys hitchhiking with tall sticks in their hands. Only we need the sticks to help us climb the hills. And ain't nothing we can do about being black, or about the fact that we got baggy, red eyes from not hardly sleeping three nights in a row. This here's farm country, so it ain't our fault either that people slam doors in our faces soon as they open them and see what we look like. Only maybe it is a little bit Kee-lee's fault. When we got to the second farm, instead of saying hello when the door opened, he said, "You got any food, lady? Any money?" The woman slammed

the door. So did the next lady. So we still out here—
ducking from police cars. Hungry. Not in no real bad
mood though, 'cause when it's daylight, it's not that
bad. We wrestle. We race each other up the road, or
beat rows of corn with sticks and pretend it's my dad's
head we're whupping. But we stay hungry even
though one lady does fix us a sandwich, though she
makes sure we ain't eat it on her property.

We're by the shoulder of the road, kicking gravel
and trying to get truckers to blow their horns. "I'll race
you," Kee-lee says. "Ready. Set . . ."

"Go!" we both say, balling up our fists, straight-
ening our backs and running up the road like
somebody's handing out free sneakers.

Kee-lee's in front at first. Then it's me, sticking my
legs way out, throwing my elbows back and smiling
when the trucker yells, "Take 'im. Take 'im. You know
you can take 'im."

Kee-lee gives the guy the finger. And just when
I'm set to pass him, he gets ahead of me, pushing me
into the middle of the road right when a beat-down
black pickup truck goes by. The driver swerves. He
almost rolls over my foot. I fall to the ground. Kee-lee
comes to check on me. I jump up and take off running fast as I can. Laughing. Smelling something

sweet like apples or peaches even. That's when I see the sign. FINNEGAN'S APPLE ORCHARD. I don't tell Kee-lee nothing. I fly across the road, looking to my left at rows and rows of short, leafy green trees with fruit hanging from them. Ignoring Kee-lee. Licking my lips. Rubbing sweat off my neck and arms. Thinking about all that fruit. "So that's what a real apple tree looks like, huh, Kee-lee?" I slow up.

"I . . . I . . ." Kee-lee can't hardly breathe.

We're sitting on the guardrail, fanning car smoke out our faces, staring at trees. "I bet. I bet they taste good."

He looks at the trees. There're rows and rows of them. "Real good."

I look at Kee-lee. "It ain't chicken."

He laughs. "Gonna taste like chicken to me."

We both step over the railing at the same time, dropping our stuff and running through hard brown grass that crunches under our feet like dry macaroni. Kee-lee bites into an apple and drops it to the ground. "Now that's what I'm talking about." He snatches another one off the tree. I'm doing the same thing: grabbing, biting, dropping, and swallowing sweet, juicy chunks so big they stick in my throat. It ain't chicken, but it sure is good.

Chapter 33

"**W**E GOTTA GO."

"I know."

"Now," Kee-lee tells me.

"I know. But I can't. Not yet."

I'm standing next to an apple tree with my pants pulled down. I got the runs. Been going for forty-five minutes and I ain't got no more toilet paper—just leaves that itch and burn me. Only I can't scratch because I can't stop going, and going is making my insides bubbly and that's making me fart and it's stinking out here real bad. "Kee-lee. I need some water." My lips are cracked and dry.

"I ain't coming over there," Kee-lee says, squeezing his nose. "You stink."

I'm rocking, rubbing my stomach. "I think something was in them apples."

He says he ate them and he's not sick. He digs in his bag and pulls out his last reefer. Things been so crazy, he forgot about getting high. "Smoke this. You'll feel better."

I tell him no. He lights up. Lies back on the hill. Looks at the sky and listens to me fart and poop and "Aaaahhhhh." I hold my stomach. Feel my insides twist and knot and squeeze. I'm thinking that maybe the farmer put something bad on 'em so kids wouldn't steal 'em.

Kee-lee's opening his backpack, pulling out paper and paints. "I'm gonna paint you. Right under that tree."

"Don't you . . ."

"Gonna call it, *Boy Crapping Under Apple Tree.*"

"You ain't got—you ain't got . . . aaaaaah. Kee-lee. Kee-lee. It hurts, man."

Kee-lee thinks it's funny. He's sitting on the hill with the sun behind him. Using water from the creek to wet his brushes and water the paints. He's smoking weed, leaning his head sideways. Telling me he's gonna get this just right.

My stomach starts up again. Kee-lee says for me to stop crying. "Babies get the runs all the time and they don't die from it." He walks over and hands me a bottle of water he filled at the creek. "Wash your hands when you done. They got stuff on 'em."

I look at my fingers, at the leaves and crap on the ground. I pour the water over my head and lick it off my lips. I wash my hands, then drink the rest. But that just makes my stomach cramp more. But a few minutes later I'm better, so I walk over and lie down by Kee-lee.

"I need real food," he says. "Apples ain't roast beef, you know."

I hear him talking, but my eyes are closing. And when I wake up two hours later, the sun's almost down.

"Mann," he says, pushing me. "Look what I done."

I push him away.

"Look."

"I don't wanna see me under no tree with my pants pulled down."

"Look."

I turn his way. There's a zillion bushy green trees covered with apples. "You like apple trees?"

"I don't know. I never saw all that many before, until now."

His apple trees ain't exactly like the ones here. They're softer. Like watery-red teardrops. His trees are taller; stronger. And they ain't sitting on a farm, they growing outta concrete right next to my house and his. They sitting on rooftops. Pushing right through people's ceilings and growing in stores that sell sweet potatoes and chewing gum, Mary Jane candies and forties. It sounds funny. But it looks kinda nice. "What you call it?"

He holds the painting up to the sun and stares. *Stone Apples.*

"What?"

Kee-lee points to the cracked pavement, then to a boy sitting on the steps playing with a gun.

"Oh. I missed him."

The boy's smoking weed and sitting under an apple tree that's got long skinny branches hanging so low he can pick one of them juicy red apples off and eat it, if he wants.

"Nice," I say, feeling my stomach bubble. "What you gonna paint next?"

His fingers are green. His T-shirt's got brown and red stains on it. We're running outta paper. He picks up the last piece and looks at me.

I say, "Go ahead."

Kee-lee's brush moves across the paper and a lake shows up. Red birds fly and bluebirds stick their beaks down their kids' throats, feeding 'em worms. His brush shakes and raindrops fall. It scratches the paper and dips in the water and the sky turns dark blue and the moon gets as yellow as a lemon iced cookie. He's quiet a long time. And when he's done, I sit straight up. It's his best picture ever. "Save it. Show Mr. Titchner when school starts back up." Titchner's our art teacher. He said that Kee-lee's the fastest painter he knows. "And when you're done," he said once, "you leave mini masterpieces behind."

Kee-lee must be tired, 'cause for a while he lets that one slide. Or maybe he just can't talk, like me, only watch the sun setting and the whole sky burning reddish orange, making the apples look like they on fire.

Kee-lee sticks the picture on a branch. "Naw. I'm done with school." He sits down. "When I get back home, I'm gonna draw a bunch of these and sell 'em." He lies back in the grass. "Keisha's gonna like me then, when she sees all that dough."

I look at his teeth and think about Keisha. *She don't want you no more than my father wants me,* I almost say.

Chapter 34

T AIN'T RIGHT what my father did. It's been more than a week since he left us, and we're nowhere near home. I'm thinking that even before I wake up. So when my eyes do open and it's pitch-black out, I get even madder. I feel around for Kee-lee. He's snoring. Lying right next to me. Scared like me, I bet. I blink. I listen to traffic and to my stomach growling. "Kee-lee." I push him. "I wanna go home."

"Stop touching me."

I push him again. Let him know that the law don't

allow parents to make kids do nothing like this. I sit up and look around. "It's not right."

"You just figuring that out?" He sits up too. Says that maybe we should find us a telephone. He stands and stretches. Holds his arms to the sky and yawns. "We learned our lesson. Let's tell your dad that."

I follow him up the hill to the road. We jump over the guardrail and sit on it while trucks fly by. We walk in the dark for a good long time, using passing headlights to show us the way, hoping we don't end up roadkill. By the time we see restaurant signs and gas station lights, my feet are burning and Kee-lee's talking about suing my dad for abuse.

Things look closer than they really are. So it takes us another forty-five minutes to get to a town. When we get there, most everything's shut down. It's just lots of neon signs, closed buildings, and people driving by fast in cars that ain't stopping for two black boys.

Me and Kee-lee sit down on the ground in front of pumps at a gas station. We're breathing so hard you can hear us sucking in air loud as them machines that breathe for people in the hospital. "Kee-lee . . . We . . ." I ain't got air enough to say nothing more.

We keep still and quiet for a while. Then we stand up and start walking. The restaurant over there is open. It's got trucks pulled up to the back and a sign that says OPEN 24/7.

"How we gonna pay?" Kee-lee asks.

I lick my lips. "We ain't gonna eat. We just gonna ask to use the phone."

He takes off his backpack. Pulls out the brown bag and holds up the gun.

I step back.

He rubs the pistol on his leg. "I'm hungry. And I'm gonna eat."

"If you planning on doing that, I'm not going in."

He's smiling. Looking at the gun like it's a whole lot of money or a watch with big diamonds on it. "I ain't eat in too long. And I'm hungry. And if they don't feed us, or they call the cops 'cause we can't pay . . ."

Bang!

I think about Jason, dead on the porch for no real reason.

Kee-lee sees the sweat on my nose and the way I can't hardly stand up good, and the gun goes back into the bag and the bag goes into the backpack and we head for the restaurant.

The woman at the counter frowns. "Y'all want something?"

Everybody stares.

"Ma'am, can we use your phone?"

She points to the wall by the men's room. "Cost is two quarters." She turns around. Picks up two plates and takes 'em to a table where six men can't stop staring at us.

Kee-lee steps on the back of my sneakers and makes me trip. "What you gonna tell him?"

"To come get us."

"What if he don't come?"

I slide my last quarters in the slot. "He's gonna."

I'm facing away from the men, but I can feel their eyes staring through my back, hear 'em saying stuff too.

"Dad," I say, turning their way. "Come . . ."

My father hangs up the phone.

I keep talking because I don't want Kee-lee to know. "We wanna come home."

The men have lots of food: french fries and burgers, drinks big as buckets, mashed potatoes with gravy, and pie.

"We don't have any more money, and we're hungry," I say into the phone.

Kee-lee's licking his lips. Next thing I know he's got the phone. "Ain't nobody on this!" he yells.

That's when one of the men asks what we're up to.

Kee-lee steps back and asks him why he needs to know.

I speak up. "We're just talking to our dad."

The man with the long black hair and the gray beard sits his napkin down. "You hungry?"

Kee-lee tells him yes. He tells us to sit down and give the waitress our order. We run to his table. The man's fingernails are black and he smells. But he's got money to pay for supper, so that's all we care about.

Kee-lee starts ordering fried chicken, mashed potatoes and gravy, ice cream, apple pie, and fish. The man says we can have what we want. I order chicken, fries, juice, grits and gravy, only the food never comes. For a whole half hour we just watch him eat. The men at the other tables laugh and ask the guy at our table about black spots and nappy hair. He looks at us and laughs too.

This man eats real slow: one fry at a time. One bite of sandwich and he sets it down. One sip of soda and it's back on the table. When forty-five minutes have gone by, I ask how come the waitress keeps going to the kitchen and not bringing out our food.

Kee-lee looks over my shoulders. "She's just reading the paper." He shouts, "Where's our food?"

Someone says it's in the trash out back. The man across from me smiles. His teeth are yellow and broken, with one gold tooth on the side. "I'd say you could have some of mine, but ain't none left." He pushes a plate full of nothing our way.

We get up to leave, but someone says we have to pay for the food we ordered. Otherwise, they're calling the sheriff. "Go ahead and call," Kee-lee says, "so we can tell 'em how you treating us."

A trucker walks over to him. "What's your name, boy? What you got in that bag, boy?"

Kee-lee never could hold his tongue. "A gun. That's what I got in this bag. Gonna use it too."

We're going to jail. That's what I'm thinking. And my father ain't gonna know where we are and they gonna do us like they did Martin Luther King Jr. and not tell nobody for days we here and maybe even kill us. I tell him that Kee-lee's drawers are in the bag. That he wets hisself so that's how come he's not wearing 'em.

Knuckles press against my chin. "You lying to me, boy?"

Kee-lee knows this guy means business, so he

plays along. "Ever since my brother got shot I can't hold myself."

The man sniffs. "You do smell."

Kee-lee farts. He used to do it all the time in school when people got on his nerves.

The guy from our table stands. "Oh, man. You people just nasty, ain't ya?" He kicks Kee-lee's foot. "Lazy. Dirty. Nasty." He shakes his head. "Walking round with underwear that got . . ."

Another fart smells up the room. It whistles on the way out. The waitress points to the door. "Get out, you black, nasty . . ."

Kee-lee's on his feet pulling his backpack off. Only he's so mad or scared, he can't get to the straps like he wants. I get up and start dragging him over to the door. His lips are shaking. "They gonna pay for what they did."

Before we can get out, another man steps in front of us. "You got something to say, boy?" He's big and tall. He looks like he could whip us with his bottom lip.

I'm trying to push past him. "No, sir."

His arm blocks me. He wants to know if we're hungry. My answer is no, but Kee-lee says, "What you think? We still ain't ate."

The whole place gets quiet. Then the door opens wide. The man drags Kee-lee out the restaurant by the neck and the top of his jeans.

I got a sugar bowl in my hand and I'm ready to throw it. "Let him go." The bowl flies by the guy's forehead. He ducks. The dish hits the door.

Kee-lee's yelling how he ain't scared of them. How his dad's gonna come blow them away. A man bends my arm behind my back and drags me out the place. Another man pins Kee-lee's arms and pushes him into the parking lot. Their friend opens the Dumpster and reaches inside, holding his wet, drippy finger in Kee-lee's face. "Eat it."

"I ain't eating garbage."

"You stink like garbage. So you must be garbage." The man's smashing rotten food into his mouth.

"Kee-lee!"

"Shut up."

"Kee-lee!"

"If you don't shut up . . . ouch!"

I stick my fingers in his eyes. Take my elbow and shove it hard as I can into another man's chin.

"You black . . ."

Kee-lee's on the ground with some guy's knees

pushed in his back, stuffing food in his mouth. Two men stand over him. One is holding a baseball bat. The other's got his fist pulled back. Every time Kee-lee says he ain't gonna eat none, he punches him. I hear the punches. They sound like a broom knocking dust out a rug hung up on a line.

"You like garbage, don't you?"

Kee-lee says no.

Boof! They punch him in the back.

"You garbage, ain't you, maggot boy?"

"No."

Boof. Boof. Boof. Fists hit Kee-lee on his side, legs, and ribs.

Another man picks up a handful of dirt swept in a pile on the ground. "You dirt, right?" He throws it in Kee-lee's face.

Kee-lee's on his hands and knees now, like a dog. They got his head pulled back and his face pointing up to the streetlight. "Eat it." They kick him in the butt.

His hands crawl up to his mouth. His lips shake open, and black, drippy food goes down his throat.

"Good, ain't it?"

Kee-lee blinks back tears.

"You want some more, don't you?"

If Kee-lee's eyes were guns, nobody would be alive right now.

"Taste like your momma's cooking, don't it?"

It takes a while, but then his head goes up and down. His lips open wide, and in a few minutes the garbage dripping from that man's fingers is all gone.

"Spit it out, Kee-lee!"

A foot stomps down on my foot. Someone drags me over to Kee-lee. "You like garbage too, don't you, boy?"

Kee-lee's got tomato sauce on his eyebrows and mustard in his hair. His mouth opens wide and he tells them men if they don't leave us alone, he'll kill 'em. They laugh, and somehow Kee-lee gets up and pulls the backpack off. He tells them he's gonna shoot them. They still laughing. "Don't do it." I run over to him and whisper, "They'll shoot us with it."

My legs get kicked out from under me, and a man standing over me smashes cold eggs and oatmeal into my mouth. I spit it out. He holds my neck way back and squirts spicy-hot ketchup down my throat. I cough. Choke. Burn down inside. The waitress is the one who makes 'em stop. She says the sheriff's coming by to pick up an order. "He sees them here, and y'all headed for jail."

They laugh. But they do like she says. Only they don't leave us in the back on the ground. They drag us over to a truck.

"What y'all gonna do to them boys?" she says.

"Mind your business."

"Don't kill 'em. You do that and I gotta tell."

The man laughs.

"We ain't killing nobody. Just gonna do what you do to garbage, Ernestine."

Chapter 35

LL THAT NEXT day, Kee-lee and me ain't talking to each other. We take cardboard that we find in the city dump they dropped us in and scrape food off our clothes and from underneath our fingernails. We walk back to where the apple trees are. Flies won't leave us alone though. They buzz in our ears and sit down to eat stuff off our faces and socks. Beetles come too. So do other things that we can't name. I pull off my shirt first. Then my pants. Kee-lee throws his sneakers, like a football, halfway across the field. It's really hot. We are really hungry and ain't

nobody around to help us. So we eat more apples. And we poop till blood comes out. But we ain't talking to each other the whole time. We just eat, poop, and wipe. Then we lie down and go to sleep. Kee-lee will say I'm lying, but he is crying. I hear him. I don't blame him none though. We ain't got nobody but us.

The following day when we wake up, Kee-lee says we're getting home today, one way or another. I don't see how nobody will pick us up smelling like we do, but I figure we ain't got nothing to lose. So I follow him.

Kee-lee has his thumb out before I'm up to the road. Trucks and cars keep going. The ground shakes. Dirt flies into my mouth and eyes. I put my thumb out too. We stay right there for a while. Then we start walking up the road, too tired to hold our arms out the whole time. A couple hours later, when we're sitting on the side of the road, we see a police car heading our way.

"Run!" Kee-lee says, ducking into some trees; rolling down a hill with me right behind him. We keep running and looking back till the road is way behind us. "I wanna go home!" he screams. Then he has a fit. He beats a tree with his fists. Kicks the air and punches leaves from a weeping willow. I think he's gonna come after me too—only I tell him if he does, he'll be sorry.

Three hours later, when it's pitch-black, me and Kee-lee hit the road again. He doesn't say nothing. Me neither. But we is both thinking the same thing. Tonight, somehow, some way, we getting outta here.

We aren't on the road five more minutes before a car stops, and a man and his wife ask where we're going. We tell them, and just like that, we're headed home.

Chapter 36

HE FIRST THING I did that day when I got inside was call my mom. Our front door was wide open, even the security door. My dad was in the backyard laying bricks, so I walked right up the steps and went inside the house. My mother always keeps her mother's phone number by the phone, so I called her at my grandmother's house in Kentucky and told her what happened. She said she'd take the train home tonight. She wanted me to call Ma Dear and tell her and Cousin what my father did, and then go and stay with them until she got back.

"Get away from him, Mann," she said, talking about my dad. She was crying. Saying how sorry she was that she wasn't there for me. "I lost one son, trying to keep another son alive in the grave." She got quiet for a while. "I let you down. I'm sorry."

I didn't call Ma Dear, not right away anyhow. That was a mistake. I was tired and funky so I sat on my bed and took off my clothes so I could shower. Only I fell asleep and my dad found me the next morning. "Glad you home," he said, patting me awake. "Glad you safe." He pulled back the covers and rubbed my head. He walked out the room. I pretended I was asleep when he got back. He took a warm wet washcloth and moved it between my fingers, up my arms, and over my face. He talked low. Asked how I was. Said for me to tell him everything that happened from the time he left me. So I did.

"I didn't mean for it to go that hard for you," he said. He rubbed his head. He walked the floor. "But there's lions and tigers everywhere."

I didn't know what he was talking about. And I didn't care. I sat up. I told him again about the men and the garbage. He looked hurt. I told him that he was wrong for leaving me and almost getting me and Kee-lee killed. He stood there, staring at the wet cement on his shoes. I couldn't keep quiet. I got out of bed. I got in his face. I told him I didn't wanna ever live with him again. He walked over and squeezed my wrists and legs, my arms and ankles, just like doctors do. "Ain't nothing broken. Get dressed."

"You . . ." I walked over to the dresser, bent down and picked up a little metal doorstop shaped like an iron. "We thought we was gonna die!" I kept thinking, Hit him. Hurt him for what he did to you. "We didn't have nothing to eat! We slept on the hard ground and them men made us eat slop!" I never used to look my father in the eyes. Now I stared at him and didn't blink. "You don't do people like that." I dropped the iron. His foot moved just in time.

I put on some clean jeans and told him Mom was coming home and she wanted me to go to Ma Dear's till she got back. "But I ain't leaving!" I kicked my pajamas in the corner. "'Cause I live here too, and I ain't letting *nobody* chase me off."

I was waiting for my dad to deck me. Or strangle me, even. He smiled. Shook his head a little and asked if I wanted something to eat. I didn't move.

"Gumption," he said, patting my back. "Being out there gave you gumption."

I didn't know what he meant.

"Nerve. Balls, boy," he said, walking to the steps. "Get dressed. Come eat. I'll cook anything you want. Anything!"

Sometimes I wonder if my dad is missing a few marbles. He throws me out. He won't let me come home. Then when I sneak in the house and tell him off, he's happy about it.

At breakfast, him and me talked like nothing ever happened. He set my plate. He made my eggs and bacon and put honey on my biscuits. He poured my milk and sat too close to me. He didn't know, or care, that I was still mad. That I couldn't stand his rotten, no-good butt. I wanted to tell him. Show him the mark on my side where those men kicked me out the truck and I fell on rocks big as basketballs and sharp as kitchen knives. But I didn't. I kept checking him out, jumping when he got too close to me.

"It worked, you know."

I downed my milk.

"You doing what a boy should. Toughening up. Walking toward manhood." He pulled out the book on African boys. He said, when they go into the forest, they take spears or knives, nothing else. "But they come back stronger, able to protect themselves and their families."

"Some come back dead too I bet."

My dad likes to tell stories. So he told me about his father, who taught him to shoot and hunt, to make tables and chairs. I can do some of those things. My dad said he didn't know it then, but his father was laying a road for him to follow. He took a deep breath. It seemed like he wasn't never gonna let it out. "But table-making hands ain't strong enough to keep you safe around here." He went to the fridge. "Hands that fix cars and shovel dirt ain't nothing compared to the ones that shoot pistols and dig knives in people's bellies."

He didn't talk to me again till I was done eating. Then he pulled out lunch meat and bread, brown bags, and juice packs. I watched him. He got six slices of white bread lined up in a row. "Mayo. Lettuce. You like that, right?"

He whistled, breaking open plastic bags of red apples and black grapes. He asked hisself where he put a hundred and twenty bucks and how come he coundn't find the bandages and alcohol. He's putting me out again, I thought. But like a dummy I just sat there, watching. When he was done, he walked upstairs and came back down with my sneakers, socks, two shirts, and the money.

"It's time."

I let him know I wasn't leaving. He said it again. "It's time." He walked to the front of the house and opened the door.

"You made me breakfast." I walked to the door. "And you . . . Mom said . . ." I stopped and told him I wasn't leaving.

He handed me the bag. "Don't go to Ma Dear's either."

I threw it at him. "Why you hate me?"

His voice shook. "How many boys of mine you think I'm gonna let 'em kill?"

"I'm gonna get killed out here by somebody!" Kee-lee would be mad if he heard me begging. "Don't make me go. Please!"

I shouldn't have let him hug me, because I didn't even like him no more. But I was tired. My feet hurt and I was hungry all over again. So when my dad hugged me tight, I hugged him right back. He whispered in my ear, "You figure out the kind of man you wanna be, and let your feet take you there."

What kind of man are you? I thought.

He squeezed me too tight; talked too close to my ear. "You wanna be a pimp—well, there's a road that'll lead you there. Wanna be a thief, sell crack and live high and die hard—well, that road's waiting for you too."

Who was talking about crack and pimps?

He pushed me away. He told me to go now, 'cause he didn't wanna be hard on me and pick me up and throw me out the front door.

"Why?"

He just looked at me. "'Cause you soft," he whispered. "I made you too soft. Made you and Jason way too soft."

The phone rang. Nobody answered it.

"You don't toughen up, they'll kill you for sure. Mann," my father said as I was just about to step onto the porch, "Men . . ."

Men leave their children, I thought, like Kee-lee's dad did. No. They kick 'em out and don't care what happens to 'em, like mine. I turned my back on my father. "Boys ain't men, yet," I told him, walking onto the porch.

My dad didn't try to stop me. I stopped myself. I didn't wanna do like he said and go back to the camp. I wanted to go to Ma Dear's and wait for my mom. Only I was thinking, Maybe he's right. Maybe I am too soft, 'cause otherwise, how he gonna force me to go?

So I turned around. A man does have to take the hard road sometimes, I thought. But he don't have to take the one his dad picks for him. He can pick his own: good or bad, right or wrong. So I went to Kee-lee's place. His mom had spoken to my dad. So Kee-lee had to leave his house too. She almost let him stay home though, 'cause she needed help with the kids. But my father got a way of making wrong look right, and now Kee-lee's back on the streets too. Only him and me figured, since we're on our own, since we men now, we gonna do what men do: anything we want. And if anybody try to stop us, they just gonna get hurt.

Chapter 37

HEN YOU GOT stupid
parents, you don't got to listen to them. That's what
me and Kee-lee figure. So we take our money and
our clothes and we go where we want—to his aunt's
place.

Kee-lee's Aunt Mary's the one the rest of his
family talks about. She runs a number house. She
dresses like a man, acts like a man, and drinks like a
man—that's what Kee-lee says anyhow. She lives on
the other side of town, and his other aunts like it that
way. Kee-lee said they gave up trying to make her do

right a long time ago. So now, they just pray for her and send her Christmas cards every year.

When we get to her place, I'm thinking to myself that it ain't so bad. Only that thought don't stay in my head too long.

Soon as you walk in, there are old ladies knitting by the corner window. They got a big pink-green-and-yellow afghan sitting in front of them, and little flowered cups sitting on saucers. Kee-lee says they drinking rotgut, not tea.

I look at him.

"Bootleg liquor. My aunt makes it."

Men my father's age are lined up at a row of telephones, placing bets. Every few minutes one of them hangs up, and the phone rings. "That's the bookie, double checking the bet," Kee-lee tells me. Then he sneaks over to a phone and calls Keisha, but he doesn't tell her where we are.

The place looks big, since furniture you'd have in your house—coffee tables, living-room furniture, and couches—ain't here. There's just bunches of mismatched chairs, card tables, and phones. Women and men, young and old, are playing cards and laughing, and arguing over poker and gin.

"All kinds of people come here," Kee-lee says,

setting his bag down at the door. "People be in church on Sunday and here on Monday."

I walk by one lady knitting a purple scarf. She asks the guy standing near me if he's got a good number. "My luck's turning," she says, laying down her yellow knitting needles. "I almost hit last night."

Three other women are quilting a blanket. I ask Kee-lee why they here. "They waiting on the number to come out. Same as all the rest."

Music's playing. People are laughing, talking, standing, walking. There's a man by the phones who looks like he'd cut your throat though. He's the bouncer. "He weighs four-fifty. Don't nobody mess with him." Kee-lee takes out some weed and lights up.

Aunt Mary's hand comes out of nowhere and smacks it out his mouth. "You planning on staying, you better act like you know."

She don't look like no man to me. She's got on a red dress down to her knees and skinny heels tall as cigarettes. You can tell she's tough though; got a cut over her left eye and another on her right cheek to prove it. She puts her hand out to me. "Heard you wanna stay here awhile. It's gonna cost ya."

When I go in my back pocket to get money, it

all falls on the floor. A man standing by her with a cigarette in his mouth picks it up and puts it in his pocket. Kee-lee's aunt winks, and walks away.

"That's mine."

He's following every move she makes with his eyes. "And?"

He's a shrimp. Short, with a big, bald head. I'm thinking I can take him if I have to. He's thinking what I'm thinking, I guess. A switchblade comes out. "Go ahead. Try it."

I'm backing up, trying not to trip. "That's all I got. She wants me to pay to stay and I still gotta eat and . . ."

Aunt Mary takes the money out his pocket and walks off. "Thanks, baby."

I been away from home two hours and already my money's gone. I tell Kee-lee his aunt's a thief. He says she do steal a little, but she can cook real good. I follow him to the kitchen. There's a stove full of big blue pots boiling and smelling up the house something good. He picks up a lid. "She sells food too." He takes a top off another pot. "Collard greens. My favorite."

I check out the next pot. "Pigs' feet." I lick my lips, break off a toe, and suck the bone clean.

Kee-lee tells me to watch the door. Then he gets

two plates, puts a fat, juicy pig's feet on each one, scoops up some greens and more corn bread than we can eat, and him and me go out back and clean our plates.

"Here," his aunt says when we go back inside. "Try this."

Kee-lee drinks his first. "Taste like a Red Lion."

I sip my drink, then I set the glass down.

The man that always follows Aunt Mary asks if I'm a girl or something.

I punch my chest. "No, sir."

He laughs. "Sir?" He looks around the room. "The police here or something?"

"I don't drink, sir."

He slaps my back so hard I belch. "Ain't no sirs here. Just plain folk. So drink up. Be a man, Mann."

Kee-lee opens his mouth wide and pours his drink down fast. Right off I can see what it's doing to him. His words come out crooked. And he laughs about nothing.

I tell them I don't want nothing to drink. But his aunt's friend tells me ain't no boys welcome here. And if I don't drink, I can't stay. "'Cause if you can't handle your liquor, you can't handle the rest of the stuff going on round here."

I look at the old ladies, at the men lined up at the phones, and the guy jumping up from a card table yelling for folks to pay him his money 'fore he shoot somebody. I watch the bouncer, wide as a poker table, go over and settle him down. And I think about my dad. How he said for me to *be a man*. Then I close my eyes. Open my mouth so wide it hurts, and pour that stuff down my throat, even though it burns and tastes as bad as the bug spray I sucked out a can like juice when I was seven.

Chapter 38

BEEN HERE OVER a week, and here's what I figured out: they don't never sleep at the number house. People ring the bell all night long. They knock on the door and ring the phone and come and go and don't never sit still, it seems. When they ain't putting in numbers, they're playing cards. When they ain't playing cards, they're sitting around, talking, drinking, and eating.

Kee-lee and me don't do all that much. We eat, we sleep, we get high off weed we buy up the street with money Kee-lee steals out his aunt's purse, and we drink all the liquor we want. It's fun. But it ain't what my father had in mind.

"Y'all come here," Aunt Mary said this morning.

Him and me both came at the same time.

"You stink. Get yourselves some clean towels and take a bath."

I smell my underarms.

She tells us that when we done she wants us to do something for her. "Make a run."

Aunt Mary's house is next to a crack house, which is next to another crack house, which is next to three vacant houses with the insides gutted out. It's nighttime, and she's wanting us to go pick up some money for her, to walk past them houses and up the street, where dogs look too scared to walk at night.

I twist my lips to the side and whisper to Kee-lee, "Tell her no."

He says we have to go 'cause we owe her. I'm figuring I don't owe her nothing because she stole all my dough. Kee-lee don't like me harping on that fact. "You gotta pay to live someplace." He steps outside onto the porch. "So you gotta pay to stay here."

Aunt Mary follows us. Says for us not to smoke nothing, because she don't want no potheads handling her money. Kee-lee and me ain't listening.

Soon as we get off the block, we light one up. It's a fat blunt, thick as my thumb. It's nighttime, but we smoking in plain sight, laughing, just hoping somebody's stupid enough to tell us to stop.

When we get to the corner of Chase and Graham we stop and light another one up. We check out the sights, get hungry, and go get something good to eat.

Kee-lee laughs. "Now, what we supposed to be doing?"

I'm sitting on the curb with my head leaning on the light pole and my eyes closed. "I don't know."

Some guys are across the street talking loud. Pushing and punching each other. They, like, twenty-three, twenty-five years old. "Yo, punk!" Kee-lee shouts.

They say we better chill.

I yell over at them next. "Hey. What you girls doing over there?"

Kee-lee asks me again what his aunt told us to do. "I can't remember." He reaches down, picks up an empty soda bottle, and throws it across the street. "They baby, sissy girls," he says, laughing.

Weed makes you think you're tougher than you are. So I throw another bottle across the street and laugh.

We should run. I know that. But it's like my mind is saying go, but my feet are saying, *What we wanna do that for?* So I stay where I am. Kee-lee lights up another blunt, and before he even gets his first puff they coming for us. Double punching me in the ribs. Kicking us in the back when we fall to the ground and cover up the best we can.

Be a man, I hear my father say. So I'm kicking back, feeling around for a brick or a bottle to hit them with. Thinking about the whupping them white men put on me. Jumping up. Fighting back. Telling myself ain't *nobody* never gonna beat me like that no more.

Only these guys are bigger, stronger, and meaner than me, so what I do don't matter much.

I throw a punch. I duck. "Kee-lee!" I yell. "They gonna kill us!"

Kee-lee ain't talking. He's curled up in a ball, covering his head and his stomach.

Brown boots kick me in the knees. "Cops!" the guy wearing the boots says.

I hear the sirens.

He slams my head into the ground and steps on me.

"And because you got a big mouth," a dude says

to Kee-lee, "I'm taking these." He pulls off the $130 sneakers Aunt Mary just bought him.

The guy beating on me stops. "I don't wear cheap shoes," he says, kicking my foot and taking off.

I'm holding my stomach. Holding my head. Listening to the blood in my ears roar. I get to my feet. "Cops." I'm limping, dragging my right leg and running to hide behind an empty shoe repair shop.

Aunt Mary throws me up against the wall. "Don't tell me nothing about how you got beat up. Just tell me you picked up my money."

My bottom lip is swollen. My eye's got a cut over it, and my body hurts all over. "We ain't get there 'cause—"

She pushes me out the front door. "Go get my stuff."

Kee-lee's explaining. "They jumped us."

She smacks him upside the head. Her nails leave a long red line behind. "You let 'em beat you?" She goes to stomp his bare feet, but he jumps back. "And take my new sneakers?"

Kee-lee's holding his cheek. "It was six of 'em."

My head feels like I got hit with a pot.

Aunt Mary takes an empty beer can and slams it

into Kee-lee's head. I duck when her friend reaches for me. Two big steps and he's got me by the neck though—lifting me up, watching my legs kick, and dropping me to the floor.

"Don't you ever come back here beat down." Aunt Mary's fingers cross her throat. "Cut 'em, if you have to. Shoot 'em, if it comes to that."

My tongue wipes blood out the corner of my mouth.

"But don't never come back here telling me you got beat!"

It's midnight when we go back out again. I ain't wanna go. I was scared and my face looked bad. Kee-lee and me both was limping, but his aunt said we had to have some more of the dog that bit us. So we did like she said. On the way over, I kept wondering what I did wrong to end up living like this. I brought it up to Kee-lee. He said for me to stop being a sissy. "So what if you get beat, long as you get back up and don't let it happen no more."

I'm thinking about the white men. Thinking about the guys from tonight. "That was two times in a row," I say.

Kee-lee means it when he says there won't be no third time. When we get to where we're going, he doesn't waste no time taking care of business.

He knocks on the door. "Aunt Mary says to pay up."

The woman is smiling. Almost laughing at us standing there all beat up. She points to my black eye. "Who done that?" She stares at Kee-lee's teeth.

Kee-lee tells her to pay up or he is gonna pimp-slap her. She laughs and tries to shut the door. I kick it wide open. I tell her to pay up or else. "Or else what?" She is holding a butcher knife.

We step back. *Cut 'em. Shoot 'em*, I hear Aunt Mary say. Only we ain't have no knife or gun. "Kee-lee," I say. "We better go."

"Sure better," she says.

"My aunt wants her dough."

The woman swings the knife. We jump back. "I ain't got it. I'll give it to her when I do." She waves the knife again. "She knows I'm good for it. Tell her I'll pay on the first of the month."

She tries to shut the door. Kee-lee's foot stops it though. "We ain't going back with nothing."

"Yeah," I say.

"I ain't . . ."

You don't hit women. My father taught me that. Only Kee-lee ain't got no father at home, so he don't know that, I guess. So he hits her. Punches her in the mouth like she's a dude. I try to make him stop. It's like he's getting her back for what them guys did to us. "Give me the money," he says, kicking her legs. "Now!"

His fingers go around her throat. The knife she's got in her hands falls to the floor. I'm pulling him off her. "Let her go, Kee-lee."

Kee-lee says he ain't letting no one hit him no more. He tells me to go inside and look around for the money. I do what he says, excusing myself for walking in front of the television the kids are watching. I bring out a tan straw pocketbook. Ten bucks is in it.

He turns her loose. She's breathing like she ain't got but one more breath left.

"Let's go," I say.

He walks in the kitchen, dumping out flour cans and sugar bowls. Digging in her freezer and emptying out cereal boxes.

The woman's got herself together now. "Boy, if you don't . . ."

Kee-lee shouts so loud he drowns out the TV. "I ain't no boy!" He runs into her bedroom and comes out with a dresser drawer. "Thought you ain't have no money? Thought you was broke?" He takes out the money and throws the drawer at the TV.

I'm looking at Kee-lee because he's smiling, liking what he's doing—knocking cereal bowls out the kids' hands and stepping on their toys. I'm listening to their mother tell them to call the cops.

He laughs. "Call 'em. They just might get here next week."

On the way home, Kee-lee's making up raps about stealing money and smashing knees. "Next time," he says, "I might just really hurt somebody."

E WAS BORED, so Kee-lee called Keisha again. He told her about the money he's making, and how he can smoke all the weed he wants. Then he asked her, just about begged her, to let him come visit. "I don't care if I get in trouble neither," he said to her. No. Keisha always says no. Only it's taking her longer and longer to get to no— fifteen minutes the first time. A whole hour the last time they spoke. "I keep telling that girl," Kee-lee said, "she gonna be my wife."

Yesterday he snuck off to meet Keisha

someplace. He came back and didn't talk to me the rest of the day. I figured she didn't show up. She did. Then I figured she wouldn't talk to him, or kiss him like he wanted. She did that too. It turned out that Kee-lee was just mad: mad at his mom, at my dad, at everybody. "She likes me now, and I can't go back home and see her like I want."

I told Kee-lee he should just go, forget about his mother and just go. "Why don't you go then?" he said.

I went outside and lit up a blunt. I called home. It was the first time I called home since coming here weeks ago. I didn't want to talk to my father. I wanted to talk to my mom. She didn't answer. He did. But he knew it was me. "Mann. I been thinking."

I don't care nothing about what he thinks anymore. So I hung up and tried to forget that I had a stupid father, a crazy mother, and no place to live anymore.

It's September. School started three weeks ago. I think about what the kids at school are doing. What they're eating for lunch and stuff. I don't tell Kee-lee. He never did like school. But getting high and doing nothing all day ain't much fun neither. "Kee-lee," I say, "I wanna paint something."

He tells me to go back to sleep. Me and him sleep on the floor, on the second floor right by his aunt's room. The wallpaper is brown and peeling off like burned skin. "I ain't painted since we got here four weeks ago. I need to though."

He turns over. I get up and go downstairs. It's five in the morning and his aunt's still up. There's a whole table full of people eating breakfast and playing cards. "What you want, Mann?'

"Paint."

"Huh?"

"I wanna paint something."

"Whole house needs painting," someone says, laughing.

"Don't need no paint. Need a bomb. Boom!" her boyfriend says, shaking the table with his hands. "Maybe that way the roaches'll die and the stink of this place will go away."

His aunt splashes her drink in his face. He gets up, mad. "Woman, I'll . . ."

"You wanna get cut?" she says, reaching under her blouse. "I ain't cut nobody in a while. Needles needs a little blood," she says, pressing the blade to her lips.

There's paint in the basement. Buckets of old

paint with thick skins on top. I pull back the skins and stir up the watery paint. "You'll do," I say, pouring some in an empty egg carton. I got yellow, dark blue, green, orange, and purple. I take the paints upstairs. On the wall, I make the brightest sun I ever seen. Then there's tiny pear trees and grass, and cars and trucks rolling up a highway. I mix purple and yellow and make brown for Jason's face and arms. "Run," I say, drawing his legs, making him run in the grass. "Run," I say, thinking about what I shoulda said the day that man came on our porch and shot him dead. "Run," I tell Jason. But he just does what he did that day—nothing.

Aunt Mary says she don't want me painting no dead boys on her walls. "It's bad luck." So she makes me paint over Jason's picture. "And since you ain't got nothing better to do with your time," she says, waving her arms, "paint the whole room." She wants it green. "No blue. Make the woodwork green."

The room's got walls as tall as trees. It's gonna take me and Kee-lee two, three days to finish it. Aunt Mary don't care. She says we living here for free. "Eating up my food and drinking my good liquor." When she's almost out the room, Kee-lee says she might as well make us paint the whole house. He's being smart. But she don't care. She says that's what she wants done. "I'll get more paint. Gonna have a new place when you two finish."

"I am not Kunta Kinte," I tell Kee-lee.

He laughs and goes to the basement with me for brushes and more paint.

That's the first time we thought about running away from Aunt Mary. Only we couldn't think of where to go, so we did like we was told. We painted her house. Only we did more than we was supposed to. We drew little brown angels in the corners of the ceilings in the living room. I never told her one of 'em had Jason's face. And we drew corner boys on the wall in the dining room. One was kneeling down shooting craps. Three more was smoking weed and another one was singing to the moon.

"You boys did that?" a woman said one day. "Do mine. I'll pay."

Kee-lee and me are good painters. We get every corner. We don't drip paint on the rugs or the wood-work. We do better than some adults, and all we get for painting six big rooms and two extra-long hall-ways is a hundred bucks. Kee-lee's aunt said we shoulda named our price up front. She pulled out a stack of bills. "Here," she says, handing us a little extra. "Go rest up. I got more friends who want work done." She says we don't have to collect money for her no more. "I'm starting a new business—painting houses." She'll handle all the money and give us seventy-five percent. "That seems fair, since y'all doing all the work."

It seems fair. But I know it isn't gonna be fair. Kee-lee's aunt likes to cheat people. And she likes money a whole lot more than she likes me and Kee-lee.

 AIN'T GROWN, so I shouldn't be up at six in the morning mixing paints and smelling turpentine. Kee-lee says the same thing. But people like the prices his aunt charges for our painting. And they like how we don't just paint a wall blue, we leave something special behind.

"How you do that?" Mrs. Windsor asked the other day. "How you make him look so real?"

Her husband died six years back. She wanted his picture painted on the ceiling, right over her bed. In the picture she gave us, he had on a gray pinstripe suit and a bowler hat with a lion's-head cane in his hand. "He always had hisself some class," she said, blowing kisses up to him.

It was Kee-lee's idea to start drawing dead people. "Folks just might slide us a few extra bucks if we do."

He was right. When they seen the paintings, they cried mostly. Then dug in drawers, pockets, or bras, and stuck a few more dollars in our hands. "Shhhh. Don't tell your aunt, but this here's for you; a little something 'cause you gave me back what the good Lord took from me."

One morning, Aunt Mary wakes us up early. She feeds us a good breakfast. She says she gonna drive us to a new customer's place and for us to finish up soon as we can. "Y'all got three more places to paint this week."

I tell her that I can't paint today. My hands hurt. So do my back.

She grabs the meat behind my neck. "You a man, ain't you?" She rolls and squeezes my skin and don't care when my legs go out from under me.

Kee-lee stands up and punches his chest. "I'm a man."

She holds tight to my skin and pulls me to her. "And you?"

I think about all I drank and all I did at her place. I punch my chest. "I'm a man!"

"Then do what you gotta do."

I look at my hands. They're cracked and swollen where the lines are. When Aunt Mary leaves the room, I ask Kee-lee if he likes it here. He says it's okay. Me, I wanna go home now. I don't care if I ever see my dad again, but I wanna see my mom. Kee-lee says he misses his mom too. But he don't miss all his brothers and sisters. And he doesn't miss watching 'em while his mom's at work. "But we can't go home. 'Cause we ain't wanted there."

He ain't wanted, but I am. My mother wants me back. She's probably worried about me; Ma Dear and Cousin too. But if I go back now, my dad's gonna think I punked out. And when my mom and Ma Dear ain't around, he's gonna let me know what he really thinks of me. Might even put me out again. I ask Kee-lee why his aunt doesn't tell his mom where we are. He says his aunt can't stand his mother, so she wouldn't give her the time of day. "And now that we making money for her, she's really gonna keep her mouth shut."

There's five gallons of paint sitting by the door when we get to where we going. "This won't take no time," his aunt says. "It's a little apartment."

She's right. The apartment is small. The man only wants three rooms painted. But the walls are cracked. Chunks of plaster big as pancakes and frying pans are missing. I point to the ceiling and the plaster. "You need that fixed first."

He says for us not to worry about the holes. Just to paint around them. He's got company coming and he needs the work done today. Yellow paint bubbles and cracks right where a leak is dripping into a rusty coffee can behind the couch. I point. "You don't fix that leak, it's just gonna mess up the new paint."

Aunt Mary didn't come in the house with us. If she had, I wouldn'a said nothing, because she woulda got mad. She woulda told me to give the man what he wanted, even if he was throwing good money after bad.

Mr. Mac rides up to me in his wheelchair. "The landlord don't fix nothing here. He takes the rent. He spends the rent. But he don't use none of the money on this place." He rolls over to the can of brown water and pitches it out the window. "I been here ten years. Know how many times the place's been painted?"

Kee-lee rubs the greasy wall. "Never. Won't get painted today neither. It's got too much grease on it to hold a good paint."

I touch the yellow wall too. "Gotta be washed first."

He asks what that'll cost. We let him know we don't wash walls. "Don't plaster neither," I say.

He rolls into the kitchen. "Then don't wash 'em. Don't plaster neither." He digs in his pocket and lays money on his shriveled-up legs. "Just paint."

So we paint. We paint the kitchen peach. But the grease on the walls is so thick, the paint won't stick good. It takes us three coats to make it look like something. We want to paint the woodwork white. But dust from the floor keeps getting on the brush and making it look like the baseboards are growing hair.

After that, we quit. Mr. Mac's mad because he's got company coming—a woman friend. Kee-lee's at the kitchen sink washing paint off his hands. I'm feeling sorry for the guy. His friend's coming tomorrow. "Maybe," I say, picking plaster off the wall. "Maybe we can come back later. Wash the woodwork and finish painting."

Kee-lee says to forget it, and he asks for our money.

The guy rolls his wheelchair over to the door. "What money? You get paid for what you do, not for what you leave undone."

Kee-lee sticks his hand out. "Seventy-five bucks a room. Pay up."

He puts a twenty in Kee-lee's hand and says he ain't paying full price for sloppy work.

Kee-lee holds on to the wheelchair handles. The doorbell rings. It's Aunt Mary, here for her money. He pulls Mr. Mac up by his shirt, turns him loose and laughs when he almost falls out the chair. He's begging Kee-lee not to hurt him, and goes to his bedroom for more money.

When I open the door and let Aunt Mary know what's happening, she tells us not to leave before we get what's ours. Then she goes to her car and leaves to make a quick run. Mr. Mac takes so long, Kee-lee and me take our drop cloths and brushes downstairs and sit them by the curb. When we get back, the door's shut. I turn the knob. Open the door. Put my hands in the air. The old man smiles, points the gun at Kee-lee and . . .

Bang!

Chapter 41

RAN. I TOOK off down the stairs—flying right by Aunt Mary. She asked me what happened. I didn't answer. If I did, I woulda said they was both dead, which they was. Only I wouldn't have told her everything that happened anyhow, 'cause she wouldn't believe me. Nobody would.

See, when the door opened, Kee-lee got shot at first. The old man couldn't shoot straight. So he shot at his ear and made a big hole in the wall behind us. Kee-lee was carrying my father's gun. I didn't know that till he got mad at the old man, pulled the gun out his pants and stuck it right in his face.

Kee-lee ain't no criminal. He don't kill and hurt people. Only he forgot that, I guess, and every dollar that man had in the house Kee-lee took. All the time he was checking drawers and threatening the man, Jason was whispering in my ear, Go.

Where I'm gonna go? I wanted to ask. *Every place I'm at, there's guns and trouble and people dying . . .*

I wasn't finished with my thought before the guns went off. The old man had two guns on him, I guess. Him and Kee-lee shot each other at the same time. Blood sprinkled my hands and face like juice from an extra-sweet orange. Some was on my lips. I wiped it away with my tongue.

Go, Jason said.

I'm gonna be sick, I thought.

Go.

I sat down by Kee-lee.

Go, dog. Go.

Wherever you go around here, bad things happen. So you might as well stay where you are. Just sit, wait, and let it get you. I thought about Jason. 'Cause it's gonna get you. Can't stop that.

My father's gun was right by Kee-lee's hand. I turned away from it at first. But then I picked it up and—well, Kee-lee was gone and I couldn't go home, and even if I did go home, somebody was gonna do what I'm gonna do anyhow—shoot me dead—so I might as well just get it over with and do it myself right now. I pointed the gun at my head. Right in the middle of my forehead to make sure I was dead when I was done. *What's it like, Jason?*

My eyes kept blinking. And sweat was beading up on my forehead. *What's it like, being dead?*

Jason's all the time talking to me. But when I ask him something worth answering, he don't say nothing.

The gun was heavy. And my hand was shaking, so I put it down. But then I picked it up again. *Shoot,* I told myself. *Do it, before they do.*

I sat up straight like I was gonna get extra credit for good posture. I started to pull the trigger. Then I dropped the gun. "I don't wanna die. I don't wanna die, Kee-lee."

I don't know why, but right then I jumped up and got the charcoal pencils Kee-lee had in his back pocket. "I want some apples, Kee-lee." I stuck my finger in his face like he could hear. "And . . . and some chicken. I like chickens, Kee-lee. Live ones. Not just cut-up pieces that you fry up and eat."

I wasn't making no sense. I knew that. Talking to

a dead boy. Staying when I shoulda run a long time ago. Asking Jason to tell me what to do when everybody knows you can't talk from your grave. But that ain't stop me from jumping up and sketching a picture of Kee-lee on the living-room wall, sitting under an apple tree holding Keisha in his lap, laughing. It ain't take me no time to do it, neither, 'cause I'm good. I can draw anything, anytime, anywhere. And Kee-lee's picture was one of the best things I ever drew.

It had to be, 'cause he was my other brother, the best friend I ever had.

I wanted to sign my name under the drawing, like I do all my stuff. But I didn't, not at first. I went to the door, looked back at Kee-lee and Mr. Mac lying there in all that blood. I walked back into the room, dipped my finger in Kee-lee's blood, and wrote the number thirty-one on the wall. Nobody's gonna know what that means. But Kee-lee would. "You're number thirty-one, Kee-lee," I said, walking out the door. "Wonder what number I'm gonna be?"

Wasn't nobody in the halls. Wasn't nobody screaming about calling the police. So I closed the door; ran down four flights of steps, out the front door, and right past Aunt Mary. She grabbed my shirt. But she couldn't stop me. "Mann," she yelled. "Where's my money?"

Chapter 42

'M RUNNING MY legs off; wearing 'em out like an eraser on a pencil. But I ain't stopping. Can't stop. *Take the bus*, my head tells me. But my feet won't quit running long enough to stand still at a bus stop. "Rest," I say. But I can't. I'm scared if I do, I'm gonna be next. *Bang!*

Kee-lee and me was supposed to open our own art gallery when we grew up.

Bang!

He made me promise not to never tell nobody; not even my dad.

Bang!

"I wanna draw stuff like I see on TV," he said. "Pictures on ceilings and walls like that man, that man . . ."

"Leonardo da Vinci?"

We were at Kee-lee's house. He was down on the floor, looking up at a roach walking across the ceiling. "Yeah. Him. I wanna do like he did. Draw something nice and make people pay big-time to come see it."

Kee-lee saw a show about Da Vinci on TV. That's when he started drawing on walls. "Getting ready," he said, "for when I'm famous."

The sides of my feet burn, right where my sneaker is rubbing it raw. I keep running. I don't stop when old people block my way. I knock 'em in the side with my elbow. I don't stop at red lights, or wait for cars to pass. I jump in their way and make them break quick or swerve to keep from hitting me.

Go, dog. Go, Jason says.

My arms feel like they pulling tires. My legs feel like they wrapped in plastic and running across wet sand. But I can't stop, can't never stop, even though I don't know where I'm going.

Chapter 43

"OUSIN . . . come . . . come get me."

I'm at the pay phone on the corner of Ivy and Dixon. It's five hours after the shootings. I'm starving and tired. Scared too. I called my mom and dad at first, only they weren't home. Then I called Cousin. Ma Dear was there. I told her everything. She was crying before I finished. "Baby. Now you stay put. Cousin will come get you."

I tell her where I am.

"I didn't shoot nobody."

"Shhhh," she says. "Everything's gonna be all right."

No it won't. That's what I want to tell her. But she's old, and she believes that things get better. "Ma Dear," I say, with my eyes closed. "You think . . . you think . . . my father's gonna . . ."

Ma Dear tells me my father loves me. "This idea he had was insane. But he—"

I ask her where my mother is. How I can reach her. She says she's living at home by herself. That she's been there for weeks, going crazy trying to find me. Cousin snatches the phone. "Your father . . . your father musta lost his mind, thinking this harebrained idea was gonna work."

Cousin says he's gonna try to get a restraining order against my dad to keep him away from me. "Your mother's in agreement," he says. "She put him out when he told her what he did. She's had the police looking for you everywhere."

"I'm all right," I say.

Ma Dear's in the background saying for Cousin to stop talking and just go get me. He says he talked to a lawyer. The lawyer says they have a case, since I'm a juvenile and parents are supposed to protect kids. "Not abandon them." Cousin says now that Kee-lee's dead, they could maybe charge my father with something too. "It was his gun. So he's just as responsible."

Ma Dear yells at him to shut up and go get me now. I slam the phone down on the hook and take off. I don't know why. I don't know where I'm going. Only I can't let them send my dad to jail.

I head for a store across the street. Look around at the chips and doughnuts, chicken and cheese sandwiches sitting on ice. While the cashier rings up a customer, I suck on a piece of ice that tastes like tuna. She smiles at a guy asking about her long nails. I open the cooler. She asks the guy if he's married. I pull out two grape-juice boxes. Pick up two chicken sandwiches and a pack of doughnuts. She writes down her phone number. Gives it to the guy. I dump my stuff on the counter, dig around in my pocket like I got money, and watch the guy head for the door. The girl bags my food and tells the man that he forgot the paper with her number on it. I snatch the bag, run out the door, knocking over boxes of sweet potatoes and string beans, listening to the girl cuss me out for making her break her nail.

It's dark. I'm outside watching the stars. Every now and then I fall asleep. But then I think about Kee-lee and I'm wide awake again. They tore down the projects that used to be here, so I'm on the porch of one of the new houses they're putting up. Sawdust is everywhere. Lumber is stacked in the middle of the street like bleachers, and a cement mixer blocks off the street. Before I know anything, I'm asleep for a good long time, and it's morning.

"Hey, you. Get outta here!"

The workers are here. Three men stand over me holding coffee cups and bagels. "This ain't no homeless shelter."

A boot goes high in the air, right over my face. "You steal something?" A hand snatches me up. "Break a window?"

"Better not be no broken windows. I put them up."

I'm shaking my head no, rubbing sawdust off me like ash. A whistle blows. Hard hats push down on big heads and heavy boots stomp across the porch and down the steps. "Go somewhere, kid."

I head for the backyard, hungry, tired, and stinking. I take a leak. Stuff my hands in my pockets. Walk up the street and around the corner to a store, thinking about Kee-lee, wondering if they've found him. Hoping his mother don't take it too hard. I ask the man behind the scratched-up plastic to make me an omelet with onions and give me fries and shrimp on the side. I grab two drinks. Pick up a handful of ten-cent candy and two twenty-five-cent bags of pretzels. When enough customers come in, I sneak out.

When I'm far enough away, I sit down and rest, dumping shrimp on my fries and squirting ketchup over everything. I use my fingers as a fork, and stuff the omelet in my mouth. An orange striped cat walks over to my food. I kick it like a can. Watch it roll down the steps, hissing at me.

"I'll smash you, cat. Kill you," I say, standing up. "Kee-lee?"

His name's in the newspaper, right on the front page. I drop my fries. The cat's licking them before I got the newspaper in my hand.

TWO DEAD.
POLICE LOOKING FOR SUSPECT.

. . . . Steven Mac, 56, lived alone and often hired strangers to work for him. On the day of the alleged murder, Mac was seen opening the door to two teens. One teen, Kee-lee Jones, was found dead at the scene. The second is said to be a black youth between the ages of 14 and 18, armed and dangerous.

STORY CONTINUED ON PAGE 17.

Kee-lee's mom's in the paper. Her hands hide her face from the cameras. "'He was a good boy,'" she said. "'Never bothered nobody.'"

Aunt Mary told the cops who I was. "'Mann Adler was the one I saw running out the house. He musta done it. Musta shot my nephew dead.'"

I keep reading out loud. "'They say his finger-prints were on the gun. But my boy was scared of guns, scared of anything violent or illegal. It musta been the other boy, Mann, that killed that man,'" Kee-lee's mom said. "'Kee-lee would never do nothing like that.'"

Chapter 44

"GOT A QUARTER, mister?"

It's been a week since I read about Kee-lee. I'm on the corner, trying to make me some dough. The man with the briefcase and the brown crocodile shoes steps to the side. "No."

I walk up to a woman in a pink suit with a purse big as a gym bag. "Lady, I ain't ate in a while." I say the words real nasty, like it's her fault. She steps to the right. So do I. She moves to the left. Me too. I put my fist out at first. Then I open it wide and smile. Her high heels scratch the ground. Her fingers unsnap her purse. "It's against the law to accost people for money." She throws a dollar at me.

I pick it off the ground and keep on begging.

I call my mom. When she picks up the phone, I hang up. I call right back. She talks real fast. Says she wants to know where I am. "He's out the house now. And I'm gonna press charges for what he did to you."

She keeps on talking. Telling me that Kee-lee's funeral was real nice. Everybody came, even kids from our class. He wore white, just like Jason. And his mother put a paintbrush, paints, and a notepad in the casket with him. "Seeing that just broke you right up.

"Mann," she says. "It's gonna be all right. Just come home. Please."

I only ask her one thing: "Was Keisha there?"

"Oh, her? Yeah," my mother says. "She put something in his casket. I didn't know what at first. But later his mother told me it was a picture—the one he drew of her that day on our block."

Then Kee-lee's happy, I think.

My mother repeats herself. "Come home, Mann. It's gonna be all right."

I slam the phone down. How's everything gonna be all right? My best friend's gone. My dad's gone.

And when they find him, they might just lock him up. And me right along with him.

I go back to my corner and hustle up more money. The next man I hit up is wearing a gray suit. He hands me a buck. I ask if he's got more. He spits at my feet. I look around, pick up a brick and chase him up the street with it. "Who you think you playing with? Huh? Huh?"

If that brick wasn't so heavy, it woulda been upside his head. But I couldn't hold it like I wanted. So when I threw it, it didn't go far. "What you looking at?" I say to a woman holding her purse like I want it. Before she answers, I snatch it and take off running. Kee-lee giggles in my head like a girl. And I hear Aunt Mary saying, *'Bout time you started acting like a man.*

I had a dream about Kee-lee. The whole time he had his back to me. I kept telling him I was sorry for what happened. He sat in the corner of his room and painted a picture of his own self. He put big red wings on his back and painted a violin in his hand with a paintbrush for a bow. I told him I would make it up to him. He turned to me with this big tear rolling down his cheek. But he never said nothing. I told him I was gonna be like him from now on—not scared of nothing. The next morning I stole another purse. Three days after that, I stuck a screwdriver in some guy's back and told him I'd dig a hole in his lungs if he ain't give me his wallet. I got a hundred twenty bucks now. But that don't stop me from hustling on corners for more. From waiting till dark and grabbing pocketbooks or putting screwdrivers or broken glass in people's backs and making 'em give me what they got. My father would be disappointed in me. I know he would. But then I hear Kee-lee say, *You ain't got no father.* And I keep doing more and more stuff; and liking it, too.

I had to start getting money from someplace else. Cops started parking around where I was. I think business owners were complaining. Or maybe folks just got tired of getting their pocketbooks taken.

On this side of town, people wear suits to work too, but they ain't got as much dough. I can tell by their clothes, by the kind of purses the women carry. Even by the money they throw in my cup—quarters mostly, not hardly ever no bills.

It's late October. It's getting cool and turning dark sooner. I got me a jacket the other day and found a nice park bench to sleep on. It's under a streetlight and there's some other people sleeping round there. But I don't trust them, don't trust nobody but me now.

For three days I try to do right and beg for what I get. But all the time I'm out there, I only make twenty bucks. I still got some of what I made from before. But food costs money, and I won't be eating soon if I have a lotta days like this.

"Excuse me, miss."

"What you want?"

I don't like how she's talking to me. But I try to be nice, and smile. "I'm homeless and . . ."

Her gray eyes go from my feet to my face. "Little boy." She sounds like she feels sorry for me now. "How come you're not home?"

I shake my cup. "All I need is two dollars for food."

Her fingers move red lipstick and pink paper around in her purse. "Where's your mother? She knows where you're at?"

I lie. I tell her my folks are dead and my foster parents don't care about me. She hands me five bucks. "In a few months, it's gonna be snowing out. What you gonna do then?"

She don't want an answer from me. She's walking up the street. But she gives me an idea. So everybody I go to now for money, I tell a different story. I'm homeless. I'm in foster care and they threw me out. My folks got ten kids and they laid off so I need to help bring in money. It works. The quarters turn into dollars. People are nicer and talk to me longer. But it don't seem to matter. Even while I'm seeing sorry in their eyes, I'm wanting to hit them, or take something off them. I can't even explain it myself, but something in me just wanna hurt somebody real bad.

Chapter 45

T'S NOT SUPPOSED to be warm in October. But it's sixty-eight degrees out, too warm for a coat. All day long people have been mean to me when they should be nice since the weather's just right. No matter what story I tell them, they don't wanna hear it. They just about run when they see me coming. They push my cup away or just come right out and say for me to leave them alone before they call the cops. That kind of stuff makes me mad, so I shove the next guy I see and tell him to give me some dough. A security guard sees what I do and comes

after me. I take off, and spend the rest of the day hiding in back a building near a Dumpster.

It's late, like two in the morning. I sleep on the porch of a vacant house. It's right around the corner from a store that stays open all night. You can buy all kinds of stuff there. Weed, liquor, guns. I pay a drunk to buy me a forty, then sit on the curb and drink the whole thing, pouring the last drop out for Kee-lee. "'Cause I ain't never gonna stop missing you."

My head's spinning. I can't walk straight. But it's warm out, Indian summer I guess, and I'm still thirsty so I get the man to get me some more. He looks at me funny when I pull out my money and some falls in the street. But he picks it up and gives it to me anyhow. Then he goes inside and gets two more cans—one for me and one for him.

He don't talk much, so while we're downing beer, I tell him about Kee-lee and my dad. I thought I was making sense. I mean, the words sounded right to me. But he keeps saying, "Huh? What you saying, boy?" Next thing I know he's telling me to go home. Standing me up, letting me lean on his shoulder. Telling me he's got a son too, about my age.

"He live with you?"

"Sure do."

"You wouldn't leave him in the street, would ya? For bad things to happen to him?"

He walks me over to the alley. "Naw. Not me," he says. He tells me to stick my fingers down my throat and let some of that mess up outta me. He asks what I'm doing out so late. I don't answer. He pats my pockets. Finds the money. Holds it in the air and says, "I oughta take it. Every dime."

I sober up then.

He hands me my dough. "Go home, little boy."

I'm stuffing money in my pocket, hurrying after him. Letting him know I ain't nobody's boy. "I'm a man." I punch my chest the way Kee-lee used to punch his. Some guys standing on the corner rapping, stare. "I'm a man! Here that, punks! A man!"

The old guy laughs. "A man ain't going in no alley with a pocket full of cash with somebody he don't know." He's tall and straight-backed. "I was gonna take it." He rubs his red eyes. "But you . . . you look like my boy. I told you that. Got ways just like him."

When we're by the store again, he picks a cigarette butt up off the ground and lights it. "Get home 'fore something happens to you." He speaks to a woman coming out the store. Grabs her bags and heads up the street with her.

I get somebody else to buy me beer. I down another can and buy a blunt for three dollars. I can't hardly see straight. Walk straight either. "Spot me five?" a guy says after I've smoked most of my weed.

I stand up, arms so heavy I can't keep his hands out my pockets, or stop his boys from dragging me over to the alley. But when they're done, I'm sober. Broke and sober. A few days later, after I've hustled up enough money, I'm back on that same corner asking everybody I see to buy me some beer and blunts. Those same guys roll me *again*.

The next week, I buy a piece.

I steal the money. Snatch it right off a woman late at night walking away from an ATM machine. For one hundred fifty bucks, I get me a nine-millimeter gun. And I'm gonna do what Kee-lee would do with it: get the guys that got me.

I think about Kee-lee, Jason, and Moo Moo a lot. Can't keep 'em out my head unless I'm high. So I drink as much as I can and smoke even more. It's making me meaner though. Making me want to get even with somebody, anybody, everybody. All week long I'm walking and waiting, hoping to see the guys who robbed me. Come Saturday, I just wanna shoot somebody, anybody. That's when I see one of them, or somebody who looks like him anyhow. "Hey, you." I call him out. I walk up to him, quick. Ask him if he remembers robbing me. It feels good, pulling the gun out and pointing it at him. I like that everybody can see what I'm about to do. That I can show 'em, how I ain't no punk.

Bang!

Me and him both stare up the street to see where the shots are coming from.

Bang! Bang! Bang!

I fire back. *Bang!* The gun gets real hot, like a glass of milk heated in the microwave. That's when I figure something's wrong with the gun. More shots are fired. People take off, crawling under cars, ducking in doorways, running into the store or up the street. I run, but don't know where to hide. I'm looking up and down the street, watching. Two men with their guns pulled out are shooting at each other half a block apart. They're dressed in suits that match their ties, and wearing the kind of hats that get put in boxes when they ain't on somebody's head. *Bang!*

I slide under a silver-blue BMW.

Bang!

I close my eyes.

"Die you—"

"I don't wanna die. I don't wanna die."

I open my eyes when I hear that, because the words ain't coming from a grown man. They're coming from a little boy. He's like five years old, standing in front of the store chewing on his thumb.

The men are walking toward each other, shooting, just like they do in cowboy movies. The boy's in the middle. Standing with his eyes closed, like Jason.

"Ma-a-a!"

I cover my ears.

"Ma-a-a!"

The men keep shooting, ducking, and talking crap. The boy gets on his hands and knees. He crawls.

They shoot.

He cries.

They shoot.

Go, dog. Go.

I shake my head no.

Jason says it again. Go, dog. Go.

I tell him no. "I don't wanna die."

Go, he says. Only this time he sounds sad and scared, like he's the one being shot at.

I'm watching the little boy. Listening to him cry. Jason didn't have time to cry. They shot him and he died right off.

Go . . .

I look up and down the street.

Go . . .

I slide out from underneath the car, lying in the street by the curb. Squatting. Looking both ways. Running; low and fast. Watching bullets fly over my head. Listening . . . to 'em whistle by, low and sad, like they sorry for what they about to do.

"Ma-a-a!"

I cover his body with mine. Tell him what I wished I'd told Jason. "Don't worry. I won't let nothing bad happen to you."

Chapter 46

RAN WHEN THE squad cars came that night. I left the little boy balled up on the pavement. And I hoped that all those cops with all those guns wouldn't come after me too.

The rest of the night, while I was trying to find a place to sleep, I kept thinking that this wasn't no way to live. So that's how I ended up here, at Ma Dear's place, looking through her back window, listening. Ma Dear always keeps the kitchen and living-room windows open—summer or winter. She says it lets good luck blow in and bad luck rush out.

"There was a shootout on West Forty-Seventh," Ma Dear says, setting biscuits on the table.

Cousin sits down. "Only blessing is that Mann wasn't nowhere around." He picks up sugar and sprinkles it on his grits. "That's all we'd need. Him involved in some more mess."

Ma Dear is a looker. Her hair's dyed light brown and styled like the young girls'. Her nails are always polished and she never wears housedresses—just pantsuits. "Well, I want my grandbaby found." She sits down across from Cousin, pouring milk in her coffee. "Enough time's been wasted."

Cousin reaches for the phone and calls my mother. "She's not answering her cell."

Cell? I think. My mother never had a cell.

The door opens and my mom walks into the kitchen. Her hair and clothes look nice, but her skin looks dry and her eyes look worse than when Jason died. Ma Dear pats her cheek. "This whole mess is gonna be over soon."

For a long while they sit around talking about things. How they have friends and family walking the streets looking for me. How they are working with the police to make sure that when I'm found they don't hurt me. How they plan to make my father pay for what he did.

It's Cousin and my mother talking about revenge.

Ma Dear listens. Then says she understands why he did what he did. "He was desperate. Lost one baby and was desperate not to lose no more."

My mother is so angry she's screaming. "He didn't have a right to turn my child loose on the streets!" She's leaning on the counter, shaking her head. Saying my father took a good boy and turned him bad. "I'm gonna make sure he pays for that too."

I keep waiting for them to say where my dad is. Cousin says he saw him a few weeks back. Uptown. Renting a room. "Says he's gonna find his son."

My mother is shaking, telling them she'll never let my father see me again. Ma Dear holds her hands. She explains to her that my father loves me too. My mother pulls away. "I will find my own son. I will raise him by myself. He will turn out to be a good man." She's walking out the kitchen. "A better man than his father woulda made of him."

She walks to the front door, then comes back to the kitchen. She lets them know that she has enrolled me in school, an alternative one. She's hired a lawyer too, who met with the judge and let him know I didn't leave home on my own, or break the court order because I wanted to, but because my father forced me into it. I guess she didn't tell them that she knew about me leaving with Dad that first time. And she didn't say if my father was gonna get into trouble with the judge or not, but I could see that Cousin was hoping he would.

My mother walks into the living room again, staring at the wall Ma Dear has filled with my paintings. "I wouldn't wanna come home either," she says, opening the front door and walking out. "Ain't nothing there but bad memories."

Ma Dear asks for water and baking soda. "My stomach's upset." She stirs the white powder in and drinks up. "Semple."

"Yes, ma'am?"

"Find my baby."

Cousin wipes his mouth with a napkin and stands up. "Ma Dear. Nobody knows where Mann is."

She belches. "Not Mann. William. Find William."

Cousin makes a face.

"He's hurting too. Gotta be." She stands and Cousin pulls back her chair. "A man who—"

He throws his napkin on the floor. "He ain't coming in this house. He ruined that child; destroyed his future."

"You do the best you can."

Cousin shakes his head. "If that's the best a man can do, then God help us."

His face gets red, like he just thought of another reason to be mad at my dad. "How you give a good boy up to the streets?"

Ma Dear is up rubbing his back, explaining that there's no way to explain none of this. But she tries to anyhow. "In a garden, insects will sometimes eat, kill everything in sight. You work hard to grow your stuff. Now you watching it die right in front of you. You think, I gotta do something—anything. So you spray. You pray. You spray some more; too much maybe. And the whole thing dies." She sits back down. "You had a problem. You tried to fix it. Fixing just made it worse." She's wiping the table and shaking her head. "That's what William did; fixed it till it just broke altogether."

Cousin hugs her and leaves. After he's gone, I take off. At the corner store, I ask for paper and a pencil. I buy an envelope with a stamp on it.

To Everybody:
  I'm all right. Stop looking for me.
                              Mann

On the way to the mailbox, it hits me. I'm gonna die on these streets. And if I go home, I'm gonna die there too: inside, where nobody will see. It takes me a while, hours really, to figure out what to do. To stop being scared and walking up and down this one street like I'm casing a joint. But then it comes to me. Something I shoulda remembered long ago. I do got a place to go—and I'm going there. Now.

Chapter 47

WHEN I GET to the horse farm, I stand at the gate and stare. CLOSED FOREVER, a sign reads.

The place don't look it though, 'cause the fences always needed painting, the gate was always broken, and the grass always looked like it does now—hard and dry with clumps of overturned dirt everywhere like somebody was planning to pack it up and take it with 'em when they left.

Dream-a-Lot Stables is big enough to hold twenty houses on it—without none of them even touching.

There's four small stables, a barn, a fenced-off patch of land for riding, an office building, and a patch of trees that leads down to a graveyard nobody uses anymore.

When I was little, the horses had saddles and they kept their heads up high when you rode 'em. But the older I got, the sadder they looked, holding their heads down low, looking like they was sorry you showed up. Hope you someplace nice, Journey, I think. "You too, Kee-lee," I say, picking up grocery bags.

With the horses gone, it's extra quiet here. But it's pretty. Leaves on the trees are the color of red peppers and pumpkins. The air smells sweet and clean. And the green barn, at the end of the trail, looks freshly painted, not chipped and dusty like I know it is.

When I get to a building with the offices in it, I look inside. File cabinets are pulled open. Blue folders and papers are all over the desk and floor. Crooked, yellowed pictures of Journey with little kids on her back hang on the walls. I throw a rock through the window. Stick my hand inside and open the door.

The first room is as small as my bedroom. The bathroom at the end of the hall is dirty and there's no water in the toilet, just a big brown ring. I take a leak anyhow. I cut on the light. "No electricity." I turn on the water. "That works." I head for the couch and lie down. It's hard and itchy. I stretch out anyhow. Next thing I know, it's almost dark. I'm opening drawers, digging in cabinets, trying to find a match. There's melted citronella candles all over the place, so there must be matches.

When I find the matches, I light the candles, one by one, and sit in the window watching the sun go down. It don't take me long to realize though that I don't like being here all by myself. It's like I'm the last person on earth.

REAKFAST IS dry cereal and raisins. When I'm done eating, I head for the couch again and go back to sleep. It's like two in the afternoon when I wake up. I'm wondering: is this what I'm gonna do, sleep my life away? So I make myself get up, even though I'm still tired. I go to the side of the building and hose my hands and face. I gulp water that tastes like rust. Go to the bathroom. Lie on the floor, and before I know it, I'm sleeping again. It's dinnertime when I wake back up.

This time I don't give myself a chance to fall

asleep. I start walking, heading for the barn. I figure I'll find something there for protection—a knife or shovel. The night before, I wiped the gun clean and threw it down the sewer. I hate guns.

I never do get to the barn where the stables are. Two deer run toward the graveyard and I follow them to see if there are more. Then I head for the riding field, wondering how long I'm gonna be here before I lose my mind. I walk the fence, taking six steps and falling off, taking ten steps and jumping down. Then I'm back up until I'm halfway around and mad at myself for not being able to stay on the whole time. A stick on the ground is my sword. I use it to fence with. I duck and jab and roll in the dirt, running away from somebody who ain't there.

I am so bored! There's nothing here but dirt, trees, and me. The quiet makes my skin itch. And it makes me think too much about Kee-lee and Jason and Moo Moo.

You a baby, sissy girl, or a man? I hear my dad say, right when I'm staring over at the graveyard, listening to noises that make me hold my breath, and pick up a rock just in case it ain't deer making those sounds.

The graveyard's not big. But it looks like the kind

in the movies, with hanging vines and weeping willows. There's moldy gravestones turned over, and some so old the wind has eaten the words away so you can't tell who's buried there. I stand staring. Wondering how long it will take for my name to disappear, for people to forget about me for good.

I don't think I can do this. Live by myself with nobody to talk to. Play by myself. Go forever with no TV, no PlayStation, no CD player, no basketball, baseball, or football, no telephone, no cell phone, no girls, no movies, no friends, no refrigerator full of food, no corner store, no nothing! Spending Thanksgiving and Christmas by myself—no turkey or cranberry sauce, or Ma Dear's sweet potato pie. I'm getting outta here. That's what I'm thinking. But I can't go nowhere, 'cause anywhere I go, somebody's gonna get in trouble for it. So I sleep. I found a blanket and a pillow—I think somebody used to sleep on the job. Luckily, it's still not too cold out.

If I was home, my mother would never just let me sleep. She'd always find something for me to do, like setting the table for Thanksgiving. But here I sleep, and sleep some more; 'cause I can. 'Cause if I don't sleep, I just might go back to being who I was.

Chapter 49

AY TEN

That's what I wrote on the wall. I'm putting down the days, just in case I starve to death and somebody finds my bones. I want them to know I hung in there as long as I could.

I'm doing like cave people—drawing my life in pictures. So the wall's gonna tell 'em plenty about me. Day Three is funny. I got a picture of me holding my nose, dumping water in the toilet. Day Four shows me lighting fire to paper—because the citronella's gone—and setting fire to the couch. On Day Eight

I'm in the middle of the field with a hammer and nails, fixing the broken fence. By Day Nine I'm mad all over again so I draw me with a hatchet in my hand, chopping pieces of the office building away.

No matter how many pictures I draw, they all the same; me all by myself. If Moo Moo was alive, he would tell me what to do. But he's gone. So I gotta figure this thing out for myself.

I'd been thinking though. I can't stay here eating raisins and nuts all the time. So Day Seven I went to town. I begged for money and I bought me four cheeseburgers and some fries. Then I went to the grocery store and wolfed down three ice-cold bottles of Pepsi before I left the place. I wanted to take in a movie, but it was getting late. I went to the grocery store again. Food shopping was hard though, 'cause I was passing up watermelon and steaks, and picking up stuff that didn't need no refrigeration, like nuts, applesauce, beans in a can, Vienna sausages, and mustard sardines.

You gonna be skin and bones, Ma Dear woulda told me. I look at my pants, falling off from not eating enough.

Day Eight I went out again. Hung out at the art store and begged for scraps of poster paper. The owner said if I swept up, he'd give me a few sheets. I talked him into giving me free paint too. The colors suck—Blacken Blue, Forest Green Berry, Moose Maple Brown, Gray, Winter White, China Yellow, and Red Sea Red. "Just gonna end up in the trash," the guy said. "The last manager bought 'em and none of 'em sold." I think he gave them to me mostly 'cause he felt sorry for me. So I packed them in a box and carried them, stopping every few minutes to rest.

Day Nine it rained for a long time. I opened the blinds and sat in the window and stared at the trees. Then I cleared old pictures off a wall. Took out my new paints and charcoal pencils and didn't stop painting for eight hours straight. I didn't paint nothing my friends would like. I drew a forest first thing in the morning, with foggy yellow light shining through, and me walking by myself, dragging an empty rope. There was horses in the painting. They were drinking from the bottom of a waterfall. When I was done, I went to sleep right there on the floor.

AY TWENTY. I hate it here. I hate it here.

I write that on the wall in the bathroom—top to bottom. Then I pack up my brushes and leave. I think about my dad. So go to jail, I think. Shoot me. Lock me up. I don't care. I think about my mother. I'm mad at her too. Then I stop walking. Stand still and think a minute. She's probably crying all the time. Wondering where I'm at.

Walking, running past the front gate, I fly up the street, heading home. Thinking about Kee-lee.

Chapter 50

257

Wondering where he's buried. Thinking I'm gonna go to his grave and pour paint over his headstone and stick some brushes in the dirt and send him off right. But then when I'm almost on our block, almost home, my feet don't wanna go no farther. They fixed to the ground tight as the bolts they use to hold the streetlights in place. For a whole half hour I'm stuck. Can't go home. Can't go back to Kee-lee's place, or Cousin's neither. It ain't that somebody wouldn't take me in. It's just that, well sometimes it's better to be all by yourself than in a house full of trouble, or around people who only remember how you used to be. So I turn around and go back to where I came from.

Chapter 51

AY THIRTY

When I lived at home, my mother cleaned up our messes. We ate off the plates, and she washed them. We slept in the beds; she made them up. Now I do everything myself. I fix the food. I put the milk carton, packages of hot dogs and wings in a bucket full of water so they won't spoil, and leave it out day and night. I gather wood to make the fire that heats the pot that cooks my food out on the front porch every night. I wash my clothes and hang them up to dry. It's me in charge of me now.

I got me a routine too. I get up and wash myself and brush my teeth with my fingers and some soap.

I eat my breakfast and pick food from out my teeth with a stick. I carry a bucket and hammer over to the fence, pulling out crooked, rusty nails, banging 'em straight, then using the nails and the boards to cover the broken side and back windows of the office building.

I always take some extra wood, to paint or file down with rocks or broken glass, and make things; like a tray for eating, a step stool, or a toolbox to carry stuff in. When I'm done making things with my hands, I head for the graveyard.

I don't go in there, but I go as near as I can. Right before you walk down the stone path that leads you there, there's some half-dead trees and vines blocking your way. There's bags of garbage, a filing cabinet, old furniture, and other stuff the owner probably dumped before he took off. Nobody goes to that graveyard, but if they came, they couldn't get down there anyhow. I thought of my mom, not being able to get to Jason. I thought about Kee-lee, and no way to get to him. That's why I started clearing a path: for them.

I got me a cat named Mac. She came up on the porch yesterday. I was glad because it was Christmas Eve, and that ain't no time to be alone. I fed her raisins today. Cats don't eat raisins. She did, so I figured she was really hungry. When she went to sleep on the railing, I played marbles with stones, and beat myself at Tonk—I made the cards out of paper and drew the faces on them myself. When it got dark, I heard noises. Saw lights down by the barn. Trucks too. I went back inside, blew out the lights, and hid. When I woke up, it was morning. There wasn't nothing down there, so I figured it was the owner, taking away the rest of his stuff, or some crackhead trying to see what he could steal and sell. I didn't go down there, but the next day I did put more boards over the windows to keep out the crooks and the cold, and I finished making a knife out of wood: a Christmas present from me to me.

Later that night, I heard moaning. Things moan a lot around here: stray cats and dogs, the trees even. So I just keep painting and watching the snow flurries. But the third time I heard it, I went to the door and stood there with it wide open. Mac watched with me. The fourth time I heard it, I went back inside and I put the desk in front of the door. I stared out the window and down the hill at the graves. Then I pushed the couch in front of the desk and put some chairs on top of all that stuff.

Half the night, I aimed the flashlight at the door like a gun. The wind blew. The tree branches shook. And the moaning got louder.

Chapter 52

AC AIN'T NO kind of protection. She's a cat that limps and rubs up on you too much. But she's all I got, so I carry her over to the stables. Walking, slow as I can, stopping to pick icicles off trees or wipe dust off my pants, gets me to the stables forty-five minutes later. The noise stopped late last night. I'm checking things out anyhow, just in case.

The barn door is almost wide open. The wind is blowing leaves inside. I'm hoping I'm wrong about what I'm thinking. So I'm walking slow. Looking at a rusty feeder in the corner of the barn, pitchforks hanging from the walls, and straw covering the cold ground. I get to the first stall and stare. I walk over to the next stall, shake my head and run out the barn. My eyes follow the tire tracks leading off the property. My feet take me back inside. Journey's brown eyes are almost swollen shut. Her blond coat is bald in spots, and you can see her ribs. Her eyes roll open when I call her name. She neighs. No, cries.

"They left you, huh, girl?" I rub her belly. "They do that . . . leave when they get tired of you."

I'm pushing her, trying to get her to stand. I'm thinking, too. Wondering. When did she get here? What were they doing here last week? Trying to move her, or bringing her here? I can't figure it out. Maiden Lucy, the horse in the next stall, is in bad shape too. She used to be black. But her coat's almost gray now. And there's white stuff around her mouth, like maybe she was foaming or trying to eat the paint off the stall wall. She's lying there too. Staring at me like I'm the one who did this to her.

I saw Jason die. I saw Kee-lee die. And I ain't watching nobody, or nothing else die ever again. So I leave—just walk off and don't look back.

Chapter 53

HERE AIN'T NO calendars here, no clocks neither. So I'm always guessing days and times. Two days, maybe three go by before I go back to the barn. In the meantime, I stay inside drawing pictures on the wall by the front door. It's a picture of my house. Me, Jason, and Kee-lee are riding bikes up the street. There are peach trees hanging low, and a dirt road under our wheels. My mom's on the porch with my dad, shelling beans. Ma Dear's drinking sweet tea with Cousin. Journey's tied up to a tree in the back. She's got three colts. They're running in the grass. Nobody is sad. Nobody is scared.

When I'm done, I stand on the toilet tank and

draw on the bathroom wall. I don't think about being cold when I draw. I'm just about out of paint, so I figure it's time to get some more; to steal 'em, if I have to. That's when Jason speaks up. *Mann.*

"Shut up, Jason."

Journey's . . .

"Be quiet."

She's gonna die . . .

My hands go to my ears. His words are still in my head though.

. . . just like Kee-lee.

The bathroom mirror breaks and almost cuts my foot when I punch myself in the face.

Mann . . .

"Shut up!"

Jason's whispering. *Just go.*

When Jason got shot, wasn't nothing I could do about it. It was the same thing when Moo Moo and Kee-lee died. But Journey . . .

Go!

Journey ain't gotta die, I'm figuring. She can live, if I just do things right this time.

Journey's muscles jump when the cold water hits them. And she cries. I try to tell her that it's gotta be done. But she don't understand. She moves her head side to side and neighs. I finish hosing her down, cleaning out her stall, and I give her a drink. Then I clip a lead rope on her halter, lean back on my heels, and pull with all my strength. She's dead weight, just lying here. I rub the whiskers on her nose and put my fingers in her mouth and rub her gums for a while. She chews my fingers, like a baby chews a pacifier. "Come on, girl. Try."

Journey rocks a little. Her feet kick. I pull. Her head raises up; her neck twists. I jerk the rope. She stands. Takes one step. Shakes her head side to side. Takes another step. Then a few more. She's walking like she's gonna fall down any minute, wobbling over to the feed can and sticking her head in. Chewing on pieces of hay, she circles her stall two times, walks over to the corner, and goes down again.

I'm patting her. Praising her. "Good. Good Journey. Here." I run around picking up pieces of hay and feeding her. "We gotta get you better. Otherwise, they'll shoot you. And it don't feel good getting shot." I make her look at me. "Ask Jason. Ask Kee-lee and Moo Moo."

She's working her lips, like my grandmother used to when her false teeth didn't fit right. She closes and opens her eyes, like she's napping. I take my finger and rub green slime from her eyes. "You need medicine and food. A lot of food."

Journey was born on this farm. Back then it was a riding farm where people paid good money to get lessons. But the neighborhood changed. Owners came and went. They got worse and worse, till the horses looked like poor trash, same as the rest of us. That's what my dad said anyhow. That's what his father told him.

I go to the next stall. Maiden Lucy is in better shape. She can't stand neither, but her eyes are open. "Hey, girl." I pick up a shovel and throw poop out the door.

I walk up to her, looking down at my feet. "You gonna buy me new sneakers?" She's eating hay out my hand. "Gonna get well and ride fast and make me some dough?"

She licks her chops. Then, just like Journey, she closes her eyes.

"Guess you get real tired when you don't eat enough."

Hosing down the floor and spraying her with water makes me wet and cold all over again. I'm blowing on my hands and trying to figure out how I'm gonna dry my pants and coat.

By the time I get back to my place, I'm ice-cold and shivering—too cold to make a fire or boil water to wash with. I do it anyhow. Like a pilgrim or a slave, I gather sticks and make a fire and sit the pot on it. I strip, hang my clothes in the bathroom, and change into the only other set I got. I make myself a note. *Steal a space heater.* I tear up the note. No electricity, I remind myself. I heat up a pack of chicken-noodle soup, the last food I got. I wash my face and hands, put the hot pot in the office so Mac can sit next to it and keep warm, and I go to bed still hungry.

Come morning, when I'm done with my chores and finish making another fire, I go to the store. I'm in a hurry, so I just grab a can opener, some dog food, a few cans of sardines, crackers, apples, bagels, butter, and carrots. It's not till I'm gone that I realize how much I took.

"I got food for you." I'm walking over to Journey, opening a can of dog food. Horses are herbivores. They don't eat meat. But there was this old lady who used to come to the stables and feed her horse fish sticks. I asked the owner about it. He said it was true. Strange but true. "It don't happen often, and you shouldn't tempt nature, but every now and again, you find a horse that eats a little something like that."

I'm hoping Journey and Maiden Lucy are those kind of horses. I don't have money enough, or arms strong enough to buy and carry all the veggies and hay they gonna need to get strong fast. So I get dog food. They eat it? They like it, that's what I figure. They turn their noses up at it? Well, then I gotta think of something else.

I trash the lid and spoon food out with my fingers, mixing it with carrots, lettuce, and corn. Journey turns her head away. I pull down on her bottom lip, stuffing food between her gums like snuff. She neighs. Her eyes open wide and her brown teeth snap. The can falls from my hand and almost hits her in the head. "You wanna die? Die then."

Maiden Lucy is different. She just about eats my fingers. She finishes the can of food and wants more. She drinks the water and licks my hand and, soon as she's done, she's asleep, too weak and tired to stand. "Journey's a quitter," I say, patting Maiden Lucy. "But you and me never give up."

 TOLD MYSELF THAT I wasn't gonna steal no more, but Journey needs horse food. Not dog food. So I go back to doing what I did before— begging.

"You got any money, mister?"

Standing on the corner for three hours makes you cranky. I know I got to chill—be nice—but it's hard. It's like thirty-five degrees out. My coat is still damp and my fingers don't have gloves on them. Besides, I only make five bucks. I'm thinking I should just take what I want; to do like I did the other times and snatch a purse or hit somebody. But I don't. I try to look sadder; more tired and hungry. It works. I get eight more bucks in half an hour. Then things slow up again. By five o'clock, I only got eleven bucks, enough for a couple of bags of carrots, celery, and rolled oats; but not enough for me to eat too.

When I pass a pharmacy store window, I scare myself. My hair's a giant bush, full of lint. My face is dirty and my teeth look yellow. A woman passes by with her pocketbook hanging off her shoulder. She snaps it shut and walks faster. I chase down another woman going in the opposite direction. She cops an attitude. "Why are you walking up on me? What do you want? Money?"

"I . . . I . . ."

She's in her green purse, digging around. Saying how she hates beggars. Hates lazy people who won't work for what they want. I got my hand out, but it's like I'm waiting for her to put rotten meat in it, or spit on it. Maybe that's why I ask if she wants her picture drawn. I always got colored pencils or charcoal sticks on me now, so I pull them out my back pocket. I tell her I don't want nothing for free. I'll draw whatever she wants, and she can pay me whatever she likes.

"I don't have time."

I look on the ground for paper, or the back of a flyer I can use. "I'm quick." I reach in a trash can for a blue flyer sitting on top. She makes a face. Tells me she's not paying for trash. Then she goes in her purse and pulls out a folded-up piece of paper. "Hurry up. Do something." She's got five dollars in her hand and keeps looking at her Mickey Mouse watch. "I work, you know." She points to a tall silver building. "Over there."

The paper's the size of a letter. I sit on the cold ground and sketch her pocketbook wide open, with her office building shooting out of it like a rocket. I got the wind blowing dollar bills out of her purse and up to the sky. It's done in charcoal gray. "Well, I'll be," she says, twisting her finger around her red dreadlocks. "That's good; real good." She pulls out an extra two bucks and gives them to me. "What are you going to do with it?"

For a minute, I don't know what she's talking about. Then I get it.

She's smiling. "Ooh, so now you get it." She closes her purse. "You got skills," she says, patting my head. "That's what my baby brother would say, anyhow."

I watch her walk up the street. I'm thinking about

what she said. Wondering how much I could make drawing pictures for people. Thinking about how much food I could buy Journey and Maiden Lucy, and how I could buy me some blankets and maybe a kerosene stove too. Right when I'm trying to figure out what to do, somebody calls my name.

"Mann!"

I take off.

"Wait!"

I run in between people, ducking, jumping over things. Not looking back, so he won't know for sure that it's me.

"Wa-ait!"

I've got extra energy, even though I haven't eaten all day. I turn the corner and hide in a store. "Sweet . . . sweet potatoes, carrots . . . three pounds, and dog food, please."

I try not to think about it, but Jason says his name for me anyhow.

Daddy.

Chapter 55

THE DOG FOOD is making them stronger. One morning after they eat, I see that their eyes are clear and bright for the first time. And Journey gets to her feet for a long while. I walk her in the stall, turn her in a few circles. I sweep up her place. Put new straw down, and wonder how long it will be before she's outdoors running.

All morning I been working, trying to keep busy. Thinking maybe that would keep my mind clear. But seeing my dad made me mad. Got me wondering if he was out there grocery shopping, or buying a new pair of pants—living life like usual when I gotta live like I ain't got a real life.

Jason's always got something to say. *You shoulda waited.*

"I wasn't thinking."

He ain't gonna be mad.

I'm giving Maiden Lucy more hay and food. "Hay's running out." I sit on the stool. "He's gonna be mad all right."

Jason's running off at the mouth again. I stop him. *He's gonna say, I sent you out to be a man and look at you—mommying two half-dead horses.*

It snowed last night. Not a lot, just a little. It started while I was back on the other side of town, drawing pictures for ten dollars apiece. I wanted to charge more, but people started complaining about paying even that much. I was sitting in front of the art store, the one where the guy gave me paints, freezing. He came outside. Checked out my stuff, and went back in. Next thing I knew he's giving me a stool to sit on and hot chocolate. Then he said, "You're charging too much, little brother." He pointed. "And you need something better than trash to draw on." He handed me a pad of drawing paper and a cup full of colored pencils. "I'm expecting you to pay me back, outta your profits."

I looked at the change in my cup. I was thinking about all my responsibilities. "I need this money for . . ."

He put up his fist. I tapped his fist with mine. "I didn't say pay me back today or tomorrow. But you have to pay me back, ain't nothing free."

I made thirty dollars. I gave him back three. He told me to look around. Get myself a book. "Why?"

"Because art ain't just a way to keep your fingers busy, it's a chance to grow your mind and set your spirit free."

I had to go, so I picked up the first book I saw. I was on the bus by the time I saw that it was about Leonardo da Vinci: Kee-lee's boy. I started reading it, then gave up on it. I looked at the pictures. One made me start talking to myself right on the bus. "That's it. That's the one!" I said, hitting the page with my finger, looking at the painting Kee-lee would want me to do, so nobody would ever forget about him.

 HEAR THE NOISE and drop my book. I don't move.

It's raining out and I ain't seen the horses since yesterday. The noise is coming from the stables. It sounds like Journey or Maiden Lucy got stabbed. If they were people, they'd be screaming. Go, I tell myself, grabbing the flashlight; stuffing a hammer down my pants, wiping rain off my lips and out my eyes.

The first thing I see is the blood. It's running outta Journey's butt, dripping on the straw.

I run over to Maiden Lucy. Same thing. When I'm

back with Journey, I pull off my T-shirt to dry up the blood. I'm slipping, sliding in the wet straw. Going from stall to stall. Trying to figure out why they're bleeding, wanting to cover my ears to keep their squeals out. I stand there holding bloody rags. Shaking my head. Thinking they gonna die too.

"Mann!"

Jason says his name, not me. *Daddy.*

I don't turn around because I know what he would say. *Why you crying, you baby, sissy girl?*

He steps in front of me. "Mann."

His arms are straight out, like he's coming to hug my mom. "I been looking all over for you, boy."

I step back. "Don't touch me."

The wind blows and the barn creeks. My father's breath smokes. Journey neighs. "What's wrong, girl?" He walks over to her.

I block his way. "Don't touch her neither. She don't need you. *I* don't need you." I pat her face. "Nobody needs you now."

"Words are bullets sometimes," my mother used to say. I know what she means. I can see how shot up my father is right now.

"You wanted me to be a man," I say, walking over and opening the door wider. "I'm a man.

Don't need no father now, that's for sure."

Journey makes a noise so scary, me and my dad freeze. He runs over to her, opening her mouth even though she's snapping at him. He's feeling her puffed-up stomach and pressing around the outside of her butt hole. "What you been feeding her?"

The words in my head stay there awhile. He asks me two more times what she ate. Finally, I'm talking, walking, and letting him know how I found her half dead and starving. I let him know how dirty the stall was and how every morning I bring 'em hay and carrots. He wipes his face, smearing blood across it like paint. "Good, son."

We go to Maiden Lucy's stall. He checks her out too. "What else you feed them?"

I'm scared to tell.

"Mann." My father takes me by the arm. "I just need to know so I can figure things out."

"Dog food."

His face drops.

"Not the cheap kind. The kind that costs a buck-fifty a can."

He reaches for a box of plastic gloves, then walks over to Maiden Lucy, stands with his feet braced against each wall, and sticks his whole hand up her butt.

She squeals.

"She's impacted; filled to busting."

Farts fly when he throws out the first handful of poop. "You know that horses are herbivores. They can't handle meat."

I know. "I'm sorry . . . I was just trying to . . ."

His hand goes up inside her again. Maiden Lucy lets out a long one. Her eyes look like mine after I let a good one loose in the bathroom.

My dad's jeans are wet and bloody. His shoes too. "Come here, boy."

I walk over to him. He tells me to rub her belly. Massage her legs. Do anything it takes to soothe her. He walks over to Journey's stall. She's got it worse, I guess. He can see it in her face. He waves me over, gets me to change places with him. Stands behind me and shows me how to get my hand up in her. He wiggles his fingers. "My hand is too big. But yours . . ."

I'm picking it out at first, pulling warm, rock-hard balls out of Journey. Throwing 'em on the floor, against the stable walls. She moans, rolls her head and kicks her legs. I hold my breath. Try not to look at my fingers after my glove tears.

When I'm done, I'm bloody, wet, cold, and covered in manure. I'm ready to head for the office to wash up. My dad says not yet. We gotta stick around. "Maybe more's up there and it's gonna get stuck coming down too." We step outside the barn. He pours cold water over his hands, then bleach from a bottle he found on a shelf. "Or maybe what we did won't matter at all. And they—"

"They can't die. It ain't time for them to die!"

He closes the barn door and falls down in the straw. "Mann," he says, yawning. "I'm sorry. I'm real sorry."

Chapter 57

WHEN I WAKE up my father is sitting next to Journey, rubbing her belly. Holding hay up to her lips and feeding her. She moans. She likes him spoiling her.

He says we'll have to spend the day massaging their legs, trying to get them to stand up. When he lays his face against hers and feels her lips, her mouth opens and he massages her black gums. "How could anyone just leave a helpless animal to fend for itself?" he asks.

He shouldn't have said that, 'cause I was all right

until he did. "She's a stupid horse," I say, kicking the stall wall. "I'm your son, and you left me." I get up and sit on a stool in the corner. "You kick a kid out—"

"Mann—"

I jump up with my fist raised. "Don't talk to me!" I lower my voice. "I mean . . . you shoulda . . ."

He stands up and touches my shoulder. I push his hand away. "If it's wrong to leave a horse by itself, then what that say about what you did to me and Kee-lee?" I'm saying stuff now that should stay in my head. Telling him about the little boy who almost got shot and how I bought a gun. His face looks the way it does when he watches sad movies but don't want nobody to know it's getting to him. He can't look me in the eyes, just stares at the floor, kicking straw.

I figure I didn't have nothing to lose, so why shut up now? "I woulda come back for Journey, if I knew she was here. I wouldn'a left her here knowing she couldn't take good care of herself."

His hands go in his pockets. He starts talking about African boys. I step up to him. "I don't need you no more." I've been holding myself back all this time, when I shoulda knocked him out, whupped him long ago, and made him pay for all he done to me. I put up my fist, till I see the pitchfork overhead.

I grab it. Head for him with it raised high over my head like a knife.

My dad rarely cries. But his eyes water up and tears come like they won't ever stop. "I threw you to the wolves." He don't even wipe them off his face and neck. "I took my son, mine," he says, hitting his chest, "and I left him in the world to get eaten up like raw meat in a shark tank."

I don't feel sorry for him. He didn't feel sorry for me.

"When you done with the horses, leave." That's what I say, right before I drop the pitchfork and walk out on him.

OR THE NEXT three days my dad works
with the horses. I watch. I hand him files for their
hooves and take hay and food in to them, but I don't
talk to him. He goes to a vet and gets vitamins and
medicine for worms. He brings more food and gets
books on making horses stronger. He pats Journey
and Maiden Lucy. Walks them more and more each
day. Brushes them and whispers in their ears. He
hoses 'em down and feeds 'em carrots and tries to
make conversation with me. But I won't talk, not to
him. Not ever.

My dad sleeps on the cold floor. He makes breakfast for us on a grill he bought, and takes long walks by hisself. He doesn't shave, so he's got a beard. And we don't wash every day, so it smells around here.

It's been twelve days since he came. I wonder if he's told my mother that he found me. I wonder if he feels bad about what he did to me. "Mann," he says. "We gotta talk."

I can't talk to him about nothing. I go in the back room and lock the door. I'm drawing a picture, one like Da Vinci did. It's being done in pencil. I'll paint it later on.

My father wants to know where I spend my days. I don't tell him. But I go to the art store. I dust the shelves and empty the trash and Ryan, the store owner, lets me sit inside and make a few bucks drawing. He's showing me how to do some things the right way, like making different expressions on people's faces. I tell him about the painting I'm doing. "I'm impressed. Let me see it when you're done." I tell him about Jason and Kee-lee one day, too. Then I talk to him about my father, not everything he's done to me, but enough. "If I lost one of my babies, I think I'd lose my mind too," he says.

But he knows what my dad did to me wasn't right. "Even still," he says, "what's between a father and son can't be broken." He grabs me by the shoulder and says maybe I ought to try and work things out with my dad.

That night, I go home and me and my dad have supper together.

Chapter 59

Y DAD DOESN'T care if I
stay in the back room all day, but he wants me to
have dinner with him. I don't know how he did it, but
he got the electricity working. Now we have lights and
heat and a small refrigerator.

Tonight's supper is hot dogs and beans again,
which I am tired of. But I don't complain. I sit down
and eat. That's when I notice Jason's little men sticking out of my father's pocket. I call him on it. He stuffs
them back inside. I ask him why he carries them; if
he's the one that's been leaving them all over our

house. He finishes his supper. Then he walks away without answering me.

I head for the back room. Then I stop. "I thought it was Mom."

He pulls out a soldier. "He got his first soldier when he was . . ."

"Two," I say.

He looks at me. "Yeah. From the start, he liked them. Carried them everywhere."

He did, I say, "even to bed."

He empties his pockets. There's Jason's toy soldiers. Jason's Elmo keychain, and Jason's picture cracked right down the middle. "I kept finding them all over the house. I asked your mom if she was leaving them. She said no. Then I figured . . ."

He scratched his head like he felt stupid about what he was gonna say. "I figured, maybe he was trying to send me a message. To say something, you know."

I know. I would find the toy soldiers too and think, Jason's home. I knew it was stupid. I knew he was dead, but when I saw 'em, I thought, well, I was hoping . . .

I tell my dad what I'm thinking.

He looks at me. He whispers, while he's sitting,

falling down into a chair. "I carry . . . I carry the soldiers, just in case . . ."

He ain't gotta finish. I know what he's thinking. He carries the soldiers just in case Jason comes back. It would sound stupid to somebody else, to someone who ain't lost nobody. But if your brother died, or your mother went to heaven, then it don't sound so dumb.

My father shoves Jason's stuff into his pocket and tells me to wipe the table clean. He's putting on his jacket. Opening the door, letting cold wind blow papers around the room. "I'm gonna bed the horses for the night." He looks back at me. "Wanna come?"

"No." I don't wanna go. I wanna paint. But I don't tell him that.

He walks to the door. Right before he walks out, he tells me that he called my mother a few weeks ago. He told her we'd be back soon.

"You'll be back soon," I say.

He shakes his head. "I told her I would go to the police. Talk to the judge. Do my part."

I whisper it. "Be a man."

His head goes up and down. "Yeah. Be a man."

When he walks out the door, I head to the back room. When I open the door, they all stare at me.

Goose bumps pop up. Kee-lee would laugh if I told him that. "Only girls get them," he said one time.

It's just a sketch. I gotta paint the whole thing and move some things around. But they're all here: Jason, Moo Moo, and Kee-lee. Kelvin too. Jackie, our cousin, is handing Mr. Mac a basket of bread; and Melvin, a guy who got shot on our block for walking too close to a dude, is pouring grape juice. The table is set real nice. There's strawberries and apples, piles of bananas, peaches rolling onto the floor, and pears in one guy's hand. My dad is sitting in the middle with Jason in his lap. It's the Last Supper for everybody, including us three: Dad, me, and Cousin.

The sketch takes up one whole wall. Ma Dear, Keisha, my mother, and some other girls are angels watching out. The table is drawn outdoors, under an apple tree right in front of our house. There are people walking toward it, lots of 'em. Boys and men—each wearing his number on his chest—dropping knives and guns, bullets and baseball bats, smiling, 'cause they know killing ain't the only way.

It's three in the morning when I quit drawing and get on the couch. It's too hot in here to sleep. But I do, for a little while. But, like, an hour later, I wake up again. That's when I notice my father's gone. He did it again, I think. But when I open the door, he's out on the steps, by a campfire he made.

He hands me hot chocolate and tells me the whole story about the African boys. I don't want to listen, but I do. "When the boys turn a certain age, say your age, the men in their tribes take them into the forest for weeks, maybe months, and teach them everything they need to be men; to survive."

I look at him when he says that. I don't have to ask why he let me and Kee-lee go it alone, when African boys have men to show them the way. He explains, "I held your hand all your life. Taught you how to be a good boy; a responsible man. You didn't need no more of that kind of teaching. I needed to know you could make it if they killed me, or came for you one day."

My father finishes talking about Africans. "When the boys come back home," he says, "people in the village give them a ceremony. They paint them up in tribal colors and they dance all night long. They probably even give them special knives and spears, 'cause they're men now."

I'm thinking about those boys. Wondering what they do in that forest. Thinking about the city kids in

Africa, too. How do people know when *they* are men? I don't ask that question, though. "Do they bring anything back with them from the forest? A lion's paw? A leopard's skin? Something to show they ain't boys no more?"

He leans back, and for a long time he's eyeing the sky. It's black and full of stars. "I don't know. But you brought yourself back," he says. "That's good enough for me."

Kee-lee didn't make it back, I remind him of that. "We was like brothers. And he got killed . . . 'cause you was stupid."

My father's eyes turn yellow from the fire. "Watch your mouth, boy!" He's quiet, then talking again. "This ain't Africa and we don't live in no jungle, Mann." He goes inside and comes out with three cans of paint. "But I sent you hunting anyhow." He pops the tops off the cans with a knife. "And the lions found you and the tigers just about ate you alive." He clears his throat. "But you came back to us, to me. Alive. And I am so glad . . . that I still have a son."

He's gotta be kidding, I think.

He sits the paints down. "You are a man. You left my house a boy, but you're a man now." He dips the brush in the paint and puts yellow lines across my left cheek.

I push him away. "How come I'm a man *now*?" I am so mad I could—I could kill somebody. "I'm a man 'cause I lived in the streets? 'Cause I stole? Why I'm a man now, Dad? Huh?" I swing and just miss his chin. I swing again and my fist rolls off his forehead. "I ain't no man . . . don't wanna be no man . . . not that kind."

He dips the brush in blue paint and I feel lines go across my forehead. He sits the brush and the can down. Rips open my T-shirt and makes fat green lines and thick red circles on my chest. His voice is low and calm, like he don't want the dead to hear.

"You ain't a man because you did all those things." He turns me around and uses his finger to draw on my back. "You're a man in spite of all them things." He tells me that I've been through more than he has in his whole life. He says that I started out a boy who hated guns, and I ended up a man who hated guns. I started out loving to draw, and I ended up drawing people I love. He goes inside and comes out with bowls of raisins and nuts. "I tried to beat you down, to make you tough, to make you be like them. And you took care of horses, fixed fences, and built stools with your hands." He goes in and comes out with bottled water. "You worked for money and built a life for yourself. And I think if I left you here forever, you would do just fine." He clears his throat. "A man takes trouble and makes it into something better. You done that . . . all by yourself."

My dad holds his hand out to me. There's a paper in it. I turn away from him. It's my birthday note. Why is he giving it to me now?

"I wanted to remind you that I was a good father once." He walks up behind me. "I taught you guys to do the right thing. I made time for you and loved you the best I could."

I feel his tears falling on my shoulders.

I ask him what I been wanting to ask him this whole time. "Why? Why did you do this to me?"

He's ashamed to say, I can tell. He answers anyhow. "To make you stronger; to keep them from killing you."

My note is four years old. I gotta be careful opening it 'cause it's falling apart. I read it again, like it's my first time. *What we have is forever.* I fold it back up. Walk over to the fire and drop it, then catch it with my other hand. Jason couldn't wait till he got his note. That's why I don't let it burn.

My dad tells me he can't undo what he's done. But if I will just give him another chance, let him show me the right way to manhood, he promises not to mess it up. Kee-lee would say not to trust him. He'd tell me to kick him to the curb and fend for myself. But I like my father. Even though he did all this stuff to me, I still like that he's my dad: that I'm his son. That him and me and Jason got something that nobody can separate, or take away.

My dad sits on the steps. He stirs the paint like he's stirring beans in a pot. "A man's job is to protect his family. To make sure they're safe. Jason was my son. Mine. And I shoulda protected him—protected you too." He pulls off his shirt. "I went to work. I taught you right from wrong. I saw boys in trouble, hanging on corners and breaking the law, and I kept my mouth shut. I figured what they did or didn't do was their mommas' problems 'cause I was sure doing right by mine." He stands up and looks to the sky. "You take care of yours, I thought. You feed 'em. You teach 'em how to be men, 'cause that's what I'm doing with mine." He stares at me. "I shoulda stepped up to the plate and helped them. That way I woulda been helping myself and my boys too."

He looks at me, and for the first time, he

apologizes for what happened to Kee-lee.

"I'm sorry. He's dead because of me." He shakes his head. "He was like my son and I put a loaded pistol in his hand." He stares at the stars. "Two sons gone now." I stare at my feet.

He takes my hand and pulls it toward his face. I draw yellow swirls on his cheeks and a blue paw on his forehead. Then I put the can down, hold his arm steady for longer than I should, and I draw a soldier.

He smiles. "You are a good artist. A good son."

We don't know what we're doing. But we dance around the fire, yell up to the sky anyhow. We are both sweating and laughing, throwing nuts in the fire and ducking when they pop. My father walks over to some trees and comes back with two walking sticks. He dips the ends in red paint. He hands one to me and keeps the other for himself. We walk around the fire, not talking. We take nine steps, tap the stick on the ground thirteen times, change directions, and start all over again. I am following him. Doing everything he does. "A man should always know when to turn around and head in the right direction," he says. Then he breaks his stick in two. I do the same. He hands me the end dipped in paint. I give him mine too. "Nothing can separate us. Not even death," he says.

I am filled up inside. Too happy to talk; too excited to stay put. I jump up. "I wanna show you something," I say, taking him inside.

He walks around the room, touching the walls like they're covered in gold. He's staring at Jason. Smiling at Kee-lee. Pointing to faces he ain't seen in a while: Earl, Marty, and George—three boys from our way who was gunned down by cops when their car broke down on the wrong side of town.

It's too much for him. He turns away, shaking his head. "So many gone . . . so many . . ."

I leave him alone for a minute. I gotta take a leak. I gotta go too 'cause I'm thinking 'bout Kee-lee and Moo Moo. How they up there smiling, thinking they gonna be famous now, 'cause I got 'em looking so good.

Mann.

It's Jason. I'm in the bathroom trying to do my business and he's bothering me, just like he did when we was at home. "Yeah, Jason?"

I miss you, he whispers.

"I miss you too. We all do," I say, running back to be with our dad.